The story of the human race is that of one man and one woman. This is the basic relationship that determines the history of mankind.

These two have many names.

Here they are Piet Huygens, Lieutenant j.g. (Medic Branch) Space Corps, and Mia Mizuno, leading crewwoman, Space Corps.

These two were complete opposites, totally different in family background, education and personality, but when they met their love was complete and intense, desperate and consuming. That love altered the destiny of an entire planet, Kepler III—altered it at a time when the colonists were seeking something as important and intangible as love—independence.

Also by
Dan Morgan and John Kippax

A THUNDER OF STARS

SEED OF STARS

Dan Morgan
and
John Kippax

BALLANTINE BOOKS • NEW YORK
An Intext Publisher

SBN 345-02503-2-095

First Printing: February, 1972

Printed in the United States of America

Cover art by Vincent di Fate

BALLANTINE BOOKS, INC.
101 Fifth Avenue, New York, N. Y. 10003

Seed of Stars

They lay side by side on the narrow bunk in the cramped gray-metal box of his quarters. Naked, his long Nordic body close to hers, small, golden, doll-like, Piet Huygens felt a sudden chill as he raised himself on one elbow to look down at her.

"Escape?" he said. "Surely what you really mean is *desert?*"

Mia smiled up at him, her round, exquisite Nipponese beauty lighting up the grayness. "Desert—a word, a Corps word."

"We *are* Corps."

She reached up, her fingers caressing his cheek. "Piet, love. We are also human."

"Up and leave the Corps—just like that?"

"Just like that," she murmured.

Looking down at her, he knew that she meant what she was saying. For her it was a simple matter of feeling and truth.

"But our obligation," he said.

"To serve the Corps? To spend the rest of our lives traveling from planet to planet inside this metal hive?"

"That is what we signed for—the promise we made."

"And had no right to make," she argued. "Then, we were filled with the heroic dreams of the Corps. We had no experience of the day-to-day reality, an aseptic, sterile reality that says a man is a man and a woman a woman, but if that man is an officer and the woman crew, then it is wrong for them to follow their natural instincts."

"But still a promise."

"We didn't know what we signed for, we didn't understand," she argued quietly. "In our family, father and mother always made sure we knew what we were committing ourselves to before we made a promise. If you find that you can't keep a promise, isn't it honest to—to stop living a lie?"

In her family . . . were there really such homes, where parents and children lived together, sharing emotions, brawling, laughing, loving? She had told him many times of her family, living at the top of Fuji Tower, the nearest block to Haneda port, Tokyo, but still it was outside his experience. His reality was a big, impersonal apartment in Lake Cities; he was the only child of two academic near-geniuses who had raised him according to the book, molded him into their pattern of mature responsibility, demanding that he act logically at all times. That was his life; he knew no other. And then he became a Space Corps officer, and that was a role for which his previous molding had already fitted him, until now . . .

"What about responsibility, Mia?"

She sighed. "Responsibility . . ."

"To the rest of the crew."

She pulled him down towards her, smiling. "Who'd miss *me?*"

The tension in his mind began to ease as he moved closer to her warm body. "I would," he said.

"Well thank you, *sir,*" she said, laughing.

"I love you, Mia," he said, clutching her to him, telling himself that this was his reality, this lithe, responsive body so attuned to his own.

"Then what else matters?" she murmured, her small mouth close to his ear.

They lay together, complete, the muffled hum and throb of *Venturer Twelve* all around them, protecting them against the whirling, star-slashed terror of space through which they traveled at many times the speed of light. He caressed her back, the smooth curve of her buttocks, gently; not because he felt a rising of passion so recently slaked, but because he knew she loved to have him stroke her. Times were when she almost purred . . .

"It would have been simpler for you if you had chosen an officer to go to bed with," she said teasingly. "Lieutenant Hoffman—she's a beauty, for instance."

"But I love *you*," he repeated. "Until I met you I didn't really know what love was."

"And now?"

"And now it is different."

"But only so long as nobody knows," she reminded him. "And how long can that be? One of these times someone, some busy P.O., is going to see me sneaking in here, and then . . ."

She was right. For a month, a whole month, they had been lucky, but their luck could not hold forever. And then, for her, disciplinary action, and for him, a swift reprimand. *Conduct unbecoming an officer of the Corps* . . .

"That's why we have to do it, don't you see, Piet, love?" she said quietly.

"Desertion . . ."

"Escape—freedom to live a real, meaningful life together. No barriers, Piet, just you and I."

"But how? Where?"

"Where we are going—Kepler III."

"A colonial planet?"

"But of course a colonial planet, a new world with space for our children to grow up in, a world where they would be welcomed, not killed at the moment of conception by compulsory birth control."

Conditioned as he was to life on overcrowded Earth and in the compulsory sterility of the Space Corps the thought was a new, exciting one. Their children, his and Mia's ...

"You realize that the colonists on Kepler III are almost one hundred percent eastern Asiatic in origin?" she said.

He considered this for a moment in silence. He had tended to look upon her as a doll, a plaything, almost, in the early days of their relationship, but as he grew to know her better he had begun to recognize that beneath the fragile exterior beauty there was a will stronger, perhaps, than his own. This idea of a new life on Kepler III was no snap, impulse decision on her part, it was something she had been dreaming, thinking, planning for the two of them, because she loved him. Then surely it must be what he wanted, too?

"The Keplerians are proud of their racial heritage—Indonesians, Chinese, Laotians, Malays and, mostly, Japanese. All Keplerians, but my people, don't you see?"

"Your people, but not mine, Mia," he said.

Her mouth trembled a little, then set resolutely. *"Our* people. You are my man, and I will not be parted from you. Neither will I share you with the Space Corps and the rest of the galaxy. As for what you look like—a scrap of surgery on your eyes, and your hair blackened, and you could be a man with a Northern Chinese ancestry."

"Even so, a strange planet . . . we would be quite alone, with no one to help us."

He had anticipated a protest, but instead, oddly, she laughed. "No, that's where you're so wrong, Piet. There is a branch of my own family on Kepler."

He raised himself up on one elbow and looked down at her incredulously. By the door of the cabin, the time numerals changed to 2014 hours, ship time. "A branch of your family? But the last colonists left Earth for Kepler nearly a hundred years ago. There can have been no personal contact between the two branches for several generations. Granted some relationship exists in theory, but in practice it is surely nothing more than a tenuous matter of record?"

Now it was her turn to look surprised. "Piet, love, that is not at all so. Two, three, ten generations—we are still family. Though time and space separate us, nothing can change that. We are family, and the family will help us."

He shook his head in wonder. "You mean it. You really do."

Now she was soft and urgent. "Piet, love, until I met you, I was content with what I had. I was doing what I thought I wanted most of all, right from the time my eldest sister got a job at the Akai factory and brought home her instruction manuals. The day I opened *Principles of Electronic Circuitry* I was finished with childish books for good. But now that is changed. Now I have you, and I want to settle on Kepler III, and have your children. And if you want me as I want you, then this is what we must do."

Her assurance was breathtaking and complete, but still he could not share her faith.

"Even if your family were prepared to help as you say, I would still need a job," he said.

She laughed. "You wonder about a job? How many Earth-trained doctors do you imagine there could possibly be on Kepler III? You will be more welcome than the spring rains."

Reason told him that she must be right in this, at least. Even on Earth there were never enough doctors. On a planet like Kepler, isolated from Earth by the vast wastes of space, there must inevitably be a much greater shortage; and such doctors as there were would for the most part be Kepler-trained, without knowledge of new Earth techniques such as lay at his own fingertips. His mood brightened as he considered the prospect. Aboard *Venturer Twelve* he was merely a junior-grade Medic lieutenant, but on Kepler III he would automatically become a person of considerable importance . . . with even minimal help from Mia's relatives this must be so.

"Piet, love, what are you thinking?" she asked, a touch of uncertainty in her voice.

"I'm thinking that it will be good to be appreciated, to be something more than Maseba's errand boy," he said; "to live and work in a real community."

Her face brightened. "Then you've decided?"

"We have decided," he said.

"Oh, Piet—you won't regret it, I promise you," she said joyfully. "We will be happy together, and I will give you many fine sons."

"We must make our preparations carefully," he said. "There will be certain things to be taken with us that may be irreplaceable, medical texts, a set of surgical instruments . . ."

"And there will be gifts to be selected," she said.

"Gifts?" he looked at her, jolted out of his consideration of essential items.

"Of course—for the family," she explained patiently. "It would be unthinkable for us to appear on their threshold empty-handed. Is it not your custom to exchange gifts in this way?"

He listened with some awe as she explained the Japanese methodical madness of gift-giving; the unending reverberations of presents received and presents reciprocated. It was a game that had to be played according to the rules, sometimes even at the cost of debt and bankruptcy, a continual to-and-fro that once begun only came to an end with the death of the participants. And even then, there was the next generation. He realized that there would be a great deal he must learn if he was to take his place in this strange society.

"Then. . . ." She sat up, twisting on the bunk until she sat facing him. She brought her arms down and extended the left one towards him. She ran the forefinger of her right hand upwards from her left wrist until it rested on a slight bump just below the elbow joint. "Then there is this."

He knew immediately that she was referring to the contraception capsule implanted in her, as in every other crewwoman of the Corps.

"Your capsule?"

"Yes, Piet, love."

"What about it?"

"I want you to take it out."

He sat up sharply. "You crazy?"

"No." Her voice sank to dovelike gentleness. "Not crazy, just in love. Deeply, completely. So much so that every time we come together there's a pang, a pang which says—'All that good seed not used.'"

"But it's against . . ."

"Regulations? Piet, we have agreed what we're going to do, haven't we? Then let us make a beginning. If I start a baby straight away we shall be at Kepler in under three months, long before I show."

But what if something goes wrong, what if we are unable to escape after all? The doubts crowded in on his mind at the thought of such an irrevocable commitment, but he forced them back, because he knew that to speak them would hurt and disappoint her.

"How do you know that you'll start a baby?" he asked.

"Trust me," she said, taking his hand and placing it over her navel. "As soon as my bloodstream is free of the neutralizing hormone, I'll take your first offer. I'm fertile, love, I know it. Why should we wait—now?"

He sat looking at her silently, knowing that the decision was already made, and that he would do as she asked because he loved her, because no other woman had ever given him what she had. Before her, sex had been just a pattern of physical relief; with her, it had a new meaning, as part of a much greater, more embracing relationship. The removal of the capsule would set the seal on that relationship. But . . .

In the humming silence between them, just as the door numerals showed 2021 hours, the ship's general alarm sounded.

DISTRESS CALL—OMNIDIRECTIONAL
MAYDAY MAYDAY MAYDAY. EXCELSIOR CORPO-
RATION SHIP WANGITURU TWENTY TWO POINT
FIVE LIGHT YEARS OUT OF KEPLER III. MAYDAY
MAYDAY MAYDAY. TWO METEORS PENETRATED
HULL. EIGHT DEAD, FIVE NEEDING URGENT
MEDICAL AID. ASTROGATION COMPUTER OUT,
PROCEEDING BLIND. LOOP ROUTE FIVE FOR SOL
III. DECELERATING NOW TO POINT ZERO ZERO
ZERO ZERO FIVE LIGHT. MAYDAY MAYDAY MAY-
DAY. EXCELSIOR CORPORATION SHIP WANGITURU
TWENTY TWO POINT FIVE LIGHT YEARS OUT. . . .

The steward had removed the scant remains of the meal, and, at a glance from Tom Bruce, himself. Now the four of them were alone in the commander's stand-by room.

Magnus said, "The trouble with coffee is that it makes me think too hard about the next *real* meal. I don't suppose . . . ?"

Lieutenant Commander Helen Lindstrom, second in command of *Venturer Twelve,* opened the lid of the pot and looked inside. "I'm afraid that's the ration, Mr. Magnus," she said, with a rueful smile.

"Anything else you want to drink, it'll be recycled water." Commander Tom Bruce's flat, metallic voice was a direct contrast to the leisured, English drawl of Magnus.

"Charming thought," said Magnus, removing a cigar case from the inside breast pocket of his immaculate civilian jacket. "Well, at least we can enjoy a good smoke while these last."

Helen Lindstrom declined, as did Joseph Ichiwara, Magnus's zealous number two. She watched as Bruce took one and lit it. He was a man with green eyes and red hair beginning to gray. The expression on his hatchet face changed very little, but she knew him well enough to recognize the tension in his manner. It had become increasingly obvious during the past few weeks that Magnus, tall, dark and slightly stooping, with his air of cultured imperturbability, was not Bruce's kind of person, and she fancied that before this mission was complete she would find herself in the uncomfortable position of providing a buffer between her commander and the civilian Explorations Division officer.

Magnus exhaled a puff of smoke with a sigh of pleasure. "We may be lucky, of course. I understand that there is a certain amount of tobacco grown on Kepler III."

"Yes indeed, sir," said Ichiwara's high-pitched voice. He beamed at his chief through pebble-thick glasses. "The crop in southern Ayoto over the past few years has been quite remarkable in its quality. According to my reports the tonnage . . ."

"I'm sure you have all the figures immediately to hand, my dear Joseph," Magnus said blandly. "But spare us for the moment. Commander Bruce is much more interested in the subject of his schedule." He turned his attention to Bruce. "You were asking me earlier if I could give you some accurate estimate of the length of our stay on Kepler III, I believe?"

"Not an unreasonable request, surely?" Bruce said, with a touch of sharpness that was not lost on Helen Lindstrom.

"Not unreasonable—but I'm afraid, at this stage, unanswerable," Magnus said. "We already have a considerable amount of information about the progress of the colony, of course, and the indications are favorable towards the granting of independence. But it is a maxim of Explorations Division that all such information must be checked out and verified. That is, of course, my job. But even with my able staff and all the help that your specialists will no doubt be able to afford me, I cannot commit myself to the extent of giving you even a rough estimate. One thing I can say with certainty is that I do not intend to be precipitate in reaching my decision. The operation will take as long as I consider necessary. You must understand, commander, that the granting of independence to a colony such as Kepler III is an extremely important affair. From the point of view of the colonists themselves, this is the goal towards which they and their ancestors have been working for a hundred years. There cannot—indeed, *must not*—be any possibility of error."

Helen Lindstrom looked across at Tom Bruce, wondering if this was the moment. As Explorations Division officer in charge of the Kepler III operation, Magnus held rank equivalent to a World Supreme Court judge, but here on *Venturer Twelve* he was technically, at any rate, under the command of Bruce. In many ways Magnus must be dependent on the good will and cooperation of Bruce, and yet it seemed that already, at this early stage, he was forcing the pace towards a trial of strength. Bruce was not a man used to dealing with intangibles. Abstract concepts bothered him, and uncertain estimates such as Magnus had voiced were anathema in his universe. Bruce was "all Corps," a solid, dependable officer in the old "damn-the-torpedoes" tradition, but . . .

The tension in the small room was broken suddenly, as the raving note of the general alarm sounded. Bruce was on his feet, running for the door almost before the sound had registered in the minds of the others. Lindstrom was close behind him.

Lieutenant Wiltrud Anna Hoffman sat in the duty chair above main control, in front of the screens, repeaters and command phones which told the continuing story of *Venturer Twelve*'s progress. Below her the duty crew moved, alert and ready, checking and feeding information. A cool, athletic blonde, with short-cut hair and icy pale-blue eyes, she watched and timed as full duty sections checked in on the signal board. She was not impressed by the fact that it had been her unusual duty to sound the general alarm. Very few eventualities in her life as an officer of Space Corps impressed Trudi Hoffman, in fact, sometimes, she found herself impatient with the apparent simplicity of the problem situations with which she was presented. Fortunately there were other areas of experience in which, given the right partner, one could be more adventurous. With Piet Huygens, for instance, there were times when . . .

The green light on the signal board registered "all stations manned." She punched out the time on the log keyboard. Good enough to satisfy Bruce, and Lindstrom, whose direct subordinate she was.

A tap on the shoulder, and Bruce's voice rapped: "Out!"

She vacated the duty chair for the commander and stood next to Lindstrom. She watched him check the emergency manning time, heard him grunt, and anticipated his next question by laying in front of him a copy of the MAYDAY call.

"Wangituru," Bruce muttered. "Another Excelsior Corporation job."

Hoffman picked up the reference immediately. Bruce was not likely to forget what the Excelsior Corporation had tried to do to him over the necessary annihilation of the mutinied *Athena,* but she knew that would not prevent his doing his duty in this new situation.

"Course maintained, sir," she said.

Bruce flashed her a brief, sideways look. "Naturally, lieutenant. I don't expect anyone to exceed their orders." He consulted the screen captioned *Wangituru.* At the center of the screen a blip pulsed faintly. "Huh. Speed not estimated yet? De Witt?"

"Linked with Maranne's crew, checking and recording."

"Contact message?"

"Sent, sir."

"Are they—" nodding at the screen, "—still sending?"

Hoffman pressed a switch, and a speaker relayed the static-battered message.

Bruce grunted. "Deceleration standby?"

"Activated, sir."

"Course change?"

"Coming through any second—"

A green light winked over the speaker labeled "Astrogation Main." Han De Witt's voice gave the figures.

Bruce spoke into the microphone which relayed his voice on all systems. "Deceleration coming up. Anyone with problems, speak now."

Nobody spoke.

Two seconds later, deceleration was on.

Wangituru was a big, lumbering ore freighter, almost as big as *Venturer Twelve,* but possessing neither the Corps ship's complexity nor resources. Effectively, she was little more than a huge container fitted with the necessary propulsion units, with a minimum of space devoted to the comfort of her small crew. Unfortunately it had been in this area that one of the two meteors had made its ravaging impact. Still moving at a speed of two hundred and fifty thousand kilometers an hour, the two ships hung within two hundred meters of each other, their bulks balanced in the star-pitted blackness of space.

There was a Corps saying, a saying which Bruce had turned into law for his own crew. "Get it right first time, because there's still plenty to go wrong." So, everything was right first time, under the coordination of Lieutenant Lee Ching.

Kuznetsov and his engineers were ready with replacements for outer skin and girders long before the ship achieved line of sight contact with *Wangituru*. They had all that was needed and were ready to jet across with their gear to the injured ship, suited and waiting as courses were matched and speeds equalized. Kuznetsov's men were, as always, first away, scorning the comfort of spaceboats, and using the power units of their heavy suits to propel not only themselves but the necessary materials and gear across the gulf between the two ships.

Han De Witt, the astrogator, was unhappy. Mindful of how this errand of mercy would upset their scheduled arrival at Kepler III, Commander Bruce had ordered that damaged astrogation gear should be taken out of *Wangituru* in banks and the equivalent put in from *Venturer Twelve*'s precious stock of spares. The assumption was that later the damaged gear would be repaired and placed in *Venturer Twelve*'s replacement stock, but De Witt was doubtful about the practicality of such a measure. However, he knew better than to argue. Lieutenant Maranne was in charge of the replacement operation. Her orders were clear; she was to see that the minimum necessary was done to enable the *Wangituru* to get back to Earth, nothing more. As usual, Bruce's orders were ruthless and direct.

This same ruthlessness was in evidence in the way

in which the medical side of the operation was arranged, but here the guiding hand was that of Surgeon Lieutenant George Tamba Maseba. The lightly injured were to be treated on the spot, in cooperation with the *Wangituru*'s Corps-trained sickbay orderly. The more seriously injured were divided into three categories. First were those who could be temporarily patched up and allowed to carry on aboard the ship until she reached Earth. Some of these would be fitted with limbs and organs from the replacement banks on *Venturer Twelve* and would, within a few weeks, be fit for light duties. Then there were those whose condition warranted mercy killing, and those who were already dead . . . these two latter classes had their own special importance.

Lieutenant Maseba was discussing the dead when he spoke to Piet Huygens in *Venturer Twelve*'s Medic Center. Lieutenant Leela De Witt was standing by.

"One thing about you, Huygens, you've got the right approach with corpses, so I'm handing that assignment to you. Caiola will be helping you, as usual. That sickbay orderly on *Wangituru* seems to know what he's doing. He didn't have enough soup to bag up all the bodies, so he diluted it and made enough, hoping that we'd be in time. As it happens, we are, with a few hours to spare."

Caiola's gentle, dark brown eyes scanned his copy of the injured list, and pointed out a name which had the note "torso crushed" by the side of it. "I've packed the skinner, sir. We can never have enough spare skin."

"Right," Maseba nodded. "But first I want you to concentrate on the list of priority organs, so that if Thunderguts suddenly decides to blast off, we're making the best of what time and material we've got. Leave big bones until last, though I can do with whole skulls for pieces. And be thorough about small bones, will you?"

Caiola said: "What about Lieutenant Kibbee, sir?"

"What about him?" the fluorotube over Maseba's desk flickered, and he glared at it, as though daring it to fail.

"He'll want to do a proper space burial for the dead."

"All right, if it keeps him happy," Maseba said. "Cooperate, but do your job first. What he mumbles a few words over and pushes towards the nearest sun will be what I don't want for the replacement bank. Just wrap the remains up well, and see that they look reasonably anthropomorphic. Kibbee has imagination; he has to have."

"Sir?"

"Dammit, he has to have, and remain a priest, doesn't he?" Maseba said. "Primitive tribal rites . . ."

A buzzer sounded. Maseba stabbed a pink-lined finger at the intercom. "Yes?"

A gritty voice spoke. "Warrant Officer Panos here, sir. Spaceboat ready, all gear checked. Waiting for Lieutenant Huygens and Caiola. I'm coming over with your lot."

"Right." Maseba switched off, and said a last word to Huygens and Caiola. "Oh, and make sure that they give you a decent room for dissection. I'll save the lives of what injured I can—but *you'll* be saving future lives. Remember that." He looked hard at Huygens, about whom he was never quite sure, and was pleased to see the tall blond youngster smile.

"I always think of that, sir," said Huygens.

Caiola was looking over the list again. "There's a note here, sir, about a *Wangituru* crewwoman named Shiu Fong Fong. It says—'Save her pretty face.' "

"I will," Maseba said, "provided I can save her pretty guts."

Piet Huygens had told the truth—that when he was in charge of dissections, he always thought of the future lives to be saved. Now, as he worked with Caiola in the twenty-five-degree warmth of the room assigned to them by Sikorski, the *Wangituru*'s captain, he was for this time, at least, "all Corps," Medic Branch. He wore waterproof, stain-resistant whites, with a skullcap and overshoes of the same plastic.

Palance, the sickbay orderly of the *Wangituru,* was assisting Caiola, working with grim determination at a task that Caiola took in his stride. Strange that Caiola, a mild man who wrote poetry in his off-duty periods, should do so well in this bloody job that he had earned himself the nickname of "Butcher" among the rest of the medical staff, particularly when huge, fearless sides of beef like Engineer Lieutenant Kuznetsov had been known to keel over at the shock of something like a cut finger. But then, inside the mind, where it really counted, weren't we all different? Take Mia, for . . .

"Sir, this one is junk." Caiola leaned over a bench and wiped his red hands on a cloth.

Huygens looked at him in surprise. "That was Van Horst, wasn't it? Junk, all of it?"

"The lot. He was a drinker, but heavy. Been brewing the stuff up in secret, I imagine. If he hadn't been killed he'd have died on duty, or something. Liver like a piece of rotten leather, should have packed up weeks ago."

"O.K. Zip him up," Piet said. He glanced at the skin freezer. "You layered that stuff properly? You know how finicky Maseba is."

Caiola answered with hurt dignity. "This is my second tour of duty with the senior medical officer, sir."

So, thought Piet, screw you, Lieutenant Huygens,

sir. He recognized that the reproof was deserved. He continued his examination of a pair of hands, and decided that they were perfect. Checking the ligature labeling, he passed them over for placement in a fluid bag. As he did so he became aware that someone was standing by him.

He looked up to see Kibbee, a lean, long-faced, rumpled man of thirty-five. Priest of the United Christian Church, Kibbee was a liberal to the extent of being able to put up the right prayer for any one of a dozen religions at a moment's notice, and in the right language. For him, there was truly one God. Even the nonreligious members of the crew regarded him with some awe, because it was he who had said the last prayer for former World President Oharo, when that great and good man died in the geriatric unit on Earth's moon.

"Hello, Piet." For Kibbee there were first names only, and he remembered the first name of every crew member.

"Hello, Bill." Piet went on working.

Kibbee sighed. "Burials?"

"Soon." Piet looked at the priest with concern. "Look, we'll have them parceled up for you, all neat and ready. If this upsets you, don't come in; be sensible."

Kibbee regarded Piet's red-spattered whites with a deep sadness. "As you are?"

"If you like."

Kibbee shook his head, and his gaze swept round the panorama of gory, scientific dismemberment. "God knows if you're doing right. I don't." And he went out.

Caiola, working steadily with the skinner, remarked: "There's a good man. Why doesn't he leave things he doesn't understand to the experts?"

Piet grunted: "Like God is an expert?"

Caiola eyed his superior with a reproving glance. "You have it exactly, sir."

For a while they worked in silence. Piet found himself thinking of that brief note by the side of the injured crewwoman's name—"save her pretty face." Someone, in the heat and anguish of disaster, had found a moment to write that. Someone cared, someone needed someone else. The thought of the Chinese girl who at this moment was probably in the gentle hands of Maseba made him think of her pretty sister from across the water. Mia. His Mia. Mia, who loved him so completely that their desertion from the Corps was the only possible solution for her. It was a mad idea, without logic. But who wanted to be logical about such a love? A new life . . .

A voice from the old life called from near the door. He started, and his probing knife slipped a little. Lieutenant Hoffman, clad in blue overalls which clung to her handsome figure, addressed him coolly. "Could I have a word with you, Lieutenant Huygens?"

A voice from the past, and one which Piet could well have done without. He walked over to the door. Caiola and Palance were hidden by a store locker, but near the door a pile of souped and bagged human limbs, arranged with the careful precision of expert butchery, lay awaiting transportation back to *Venturer*.

Trudi Hoffman had been working hard; on approaching he could see sweat on the tough, Nordic features. Her blue eyes had the bite of a January frost.

"Look," he said. "You're not supposed to be in here. Kibbee must have left the door unhooked. I've got a lot of work to do—"

Her gaze roved over the heap of bloated plastic bags and their ghoulish contents, then came back to him with unshaken concentration. "As you're so good at avoiding me on *Vee Twelve*, I thought I'd run you down here."

"There's a time limit to this job, you know. I don't want to take back useless—"

"Piet!" Her voice cut him short. "We had a good

thing going, you and I. We had it every way we wanted it, and it was good. Anything you asked of me, you had; anything I asked of you, I got. Then it stopped. Why, Piet?"

He stared at her. What she said was true. Their sexual appetites had been well-matched. She had given him complete satisfaction, or so he had thought until his first encounter with the magic of Mia. Then he had been able to recognize his relationship with Trudi for what it was, a shared interest in sexual athletics in which each played nothing more than the function of a satisfaction machine for the other. Sex with Mia was only part of a much greater whole, a welding together of two personalities such as he had never before experienced, a giving and a complete acceptance. Trudi could have no conception of such a relationship; indeed, she probably had no need of it.

"I can't talk now—"

"To hell with that!" Her voice was a hiss. "I want to know. You're not making it with anyone else in the mess, I know that much, and you can't do without it this long!"

Then she didn't know about Mia. That was good. But she would find out eventually; she would make it her business to find out. And when she did. . . . He turned away from the icy blast of her gaze, and found himself staring at the result of his own butchery. What kind of woman could be so blind to the ordinary humanities that she should choose *this* scene and *this* background to demand a reasoned explanation of why he no longer wished to ride her? The dismembered dead, now destined to become so much stored material in the deep freeze banks of *Venturer Twelve,* meant nothing more to her than so many stacked engineering spares.

Hers was the Corps disease, the danger that every woman member faced, but which struck especially at the officer class with its additional burden of tradition and responsibility. In the pursuit of such a career it was necessary to forswear love. Different women reacted in different ways; some became to all intents men, their womanness dried and hardened into something beyond masculinity. Others, like Trudi, became loveless tigresses, permanently in heat, demanding the constant mechanical satisfaction of off-duty copulation as a compensation for the love they could never have. He pitied her, but he lacked the moral courage to be frank with her.

"I wanted to work, to study. I've been taking balancing hormone shots to cool me down. There's so much to learn, so little time . . ."

"Liar!" Her voice was incredulous, scathing. "I don't believe you. You would never do that—it means too much to you. There's not an officer on this ship gives it to me the way you did. You must be getting your satisfaction somewhere; why not with me?" The glare went from her eyes, and she asked, in a voice which, by comparison, was tender: "Come and see me, please, when you're back on board?"

He nodded, taking the chance to get rid of her. "Yeah, yeah, I'll do that. Now will you please go?"

She stiffened, on the brink of yet further argument, then apparently realizing the futility, she turned abruptly and left. Piet leaned against the locker for a moment and took off his skullcap to wipe the drenching sweat. Palance approached.

"Too hot for you, sir?"

"No, no. I'm O.K. How are we doing?"

"I figure we'll save all your lieutenant needs, sir."

"Fine."

Palance added his burden to the growing stack of plastic bags and went away. Piet put on his cap and glanced at the door. Even as he wondered if it was proof against further visitors, it opened.

Mia stood there, tiny and neat in her blue coveralls, with the flash of her rank on the left shoulder, her hair dank with sweat. He backed into the angle of the locker, where Caiola and Palance could not see, and she thrust herself close to him.

"Piet, love," she whispered. "They said you were working down here. We've finished up in Astrogation, and . . ."

Her voice died in her throat. It was, perhaps, not entirely credible that one of her race could ever be said to be wide-eyed, but she seemed so now, as she stared at the pile of plastic bags.

And because he knew, because he felt what she was feeling so deeply, his reply was deliberately harsh. "You aren't supposed to be in here, Mia. Do you hear me? For God's sake, girl, turn your eyes away!"

She was weeping, the sobs shaking her small frame. "Those men . . . oh, Piet, those poor, poor men!" She buried her face in his shoulder, seeking the comfort of physical contact against the horror that was beyond bearing.

"Mia, love—Mia." Now he held his hand at the back of her small, neat head and smiled down at her. "We are all poor creatures. Perhaps in some respects these men are luckier than most—because in death they will live on."

She looked up at him, her round doll-face seeking comfort from his own. "I think . . . perhaps I can understand. But I must still feel sorry for them, for what they have lost . . ."

"Then go back to *Vee Twelve* and if you wish, make a paper shrine and burn a stick for them. But be happy for them."

She nodded. "I'll try. And when *you* are back, and we are together again . . . then, will you take out the capsule?"

The need of her had him in thrall. This was no cold-minded bitch who wanted him for mere physical relief; she needed him to fulfill her creative purpose, and she gave him a love that no other woman, not even his mother, had ever given him before.

"Yes—the capsule," he said.

A sudden, incredibly bright smile, and she was gone. He returned to his work.

Back on *Venturer Twelve,* in the commander's standby room, Bruce was taking informal reports on the *Wangituru* operation. Lindstrom hovered close by, aware of his impatience to continue the journey to Kepler III.

Kuznetsov, a two-meter piece of Ural rock, was pleased and boastful. "All repairs completed. My boys did the job straight, no rest, no sick calls, no spacehead. When they got their suits off they all stank like latrines —or maybe just like engineers." He grinned at Lindstrom.

Bruce grunted his acknowledgment.

Radar Lieutenant Maranne, looking like something fresh off a recruiting poster, said: "All replacements completed, no hitches. Mia Mizuno is developing so well I intend to put in a promotion recommendation. We ought to have a larger proportion of Japanese in electronics. They're so good at it, supple in mind and body."

Magnus looked in and said: "I took the liberty of calling Kepler III on sub-etheric to explain the delay. Courtesy, you know. They will be feeling very sensitive in this, their independence year, so I felt that the expenditure in tact was quite justified."

"We'll not keep them waiting longer than necessary," Bruce said.

Kibbee said: "Captain Sikorski is a good man. We had time to do the burial service properly."

Maseba said to Kibbee: "May their spirits see God

in the light of a far sun." He anticipated Kibbee's eager response. "I mean, your God. Mine isn't so liberal. He looks at skins, and man, I'm favored." Kibbee left with a slightly bemused, somewhat hurt expression. "All items stored in the replacement bank, sir."

Lindstrom winced as Bruce said: "Fine! Now maybe you can make me those dozen extra crewmen Admin wouldn't allow me back on Earth?"

"I guess not," Maseba answered smoothly. "It seems I'd need Kibbee's God for that. Little matter of the breath of life, he'd say." He looked keenly at Bruce. "Sir, please come in for an eye check tomorrow, about twelve-thirty, or when you can make it."

Bruce stiffened. "What's supposed to be the matter with me?" he snapped.

"You come in the morning, sir, and we'll find out. Your eyes are slightly off-focus. Overwork, maybe—but we ought to know."

Lindstrom smiled to herself, anticipating Bruce's growling reply.

"I'll see if I can fit it in, if you insist."

Maseba rose, easy and graceful as a young lion. "You do that, sir." He paused at the door, a mischievous smile suffusing his ebony face. "That *is* a medical order, sir."

Lindstrom expected Bruce to snap again, but he turned his attention to his checklist, giving her an opportunity to say something that had been on her own mind.

"George."

"Ma'am?" He looked at her, enquiringly.

"That was great work you did. I saw that Chinese girl. When she gets the bandages off, is the covered half of her face going to match the half I saw?"

"Why, sure it will," Maseba said. "Why else do you think they used to call me the Rodin of the plastic surgery department back in Lake Cities?"

"I just hope you're around if anything like that should ever happen to me," Helen said.

He grinned and held up his big, delicate-fingered hands. "They're all for you, baby. Any time."

Then he was gone, and Lindstrom was alone with Bruce. She realized that this was something which rarely happened now. Once, back on Earth, before he had got command of *Venturer Twelve,* he had needed her. But now he kept his distance, and they were nothing more than commander and second in command. For him, at least, it was over. Now he worked constantly, never relaxing, maintaining the impenetrable shield of efficiency, giving no hint of the humanity that must lie beneath that hard carapace. And yet . . .

She said, aware of the touch of tenderness in her voice: "You will look in on Maseba tomorrow?"

He nodded, without looking at her, and she realized that she had failed again to make contact. She saluted formally and left.

Back in her own quarters, she showered luxuriously until the water conservation buzzer sounded, then changed into a soft, one-piece zipsuit. She rang, and a moment later P.O. Dockridge thrust his terrier head round the door.

"Yes, ma'am?" Dockridge was over-age, and with his unsatisfactorily mended leg should not have been in the crew; but Bruce had asked for him, so the regulations were bent a little.

"Two whole-wheat and ham sandwiches—and coffee."

Dockridge screwed up his face. "They'll have to be taken off your real-food ration, ma'am."

"So take them. Leave them by the door, will you?"

"Yes, ma'am." And Dockridge was gone.

A moment later there came another knock. This one she had been expecting. Sergei Kuznetsov looked round the door, beamed, came in and filled the cabin.

"Ah!" He smelled of fresh pine, and his great chest

swelled inside his off-duty zipsuit. He sat beside her, and, like a conjuror, produced a plastic bottle of colorless liquid. "See? Vodka!" His eyes shone with pleasure and anticipation.

"Sergei, where did you get it? What about Corps regs?"

When Kuznetsov shrugged it was like a small earthquake. "So? Maseba brews himself arak. And me—I was supervising engineer on the *Wangituru* job. Captain Sikorski is from Magnitogorsk; I am from Magnitogorsk. I should miss such an opportunity!"

She watched as the enormous man poured her a drink. They toasted each other, and as she sipped it, she sadly reflected that at least, with him, she could find relief and comfort of a kind.

But only of a kind.

Two themes of conversation were traditional during a junior officers' mess meal aboard a Corps ship in deep space, and both of them were treated as equally suitable subjects for obscene variations on a number of standard joke patterns. Piet Huygens remembered reading a doctoral thesis in psychiatry during his college days on the subject which went to great lengths to show reasons for the lack of originality in subject matter and form during such conversations, and to explain why novelty in any respect was by some tacit agreement considered tabu. Basically, the writer argued, the stereotyped to-and-fro of such mess conversation was an automatic response on the part of the human beings concerned to their environment. Protected from the incomprehensible, whirling horror of sub-space by only the hull of a ship, aware of the puny insignificance of his physical presence in a totally alien environment, a man—or woman—reacted defensively by exhibiting this obsessional preoccupation with two natural and ever-present functions of the human body, food and sex. Thus boredom was, in a sense, used as a protection against fear, and assiduously pursued by even the most intelligent members of the group.

At the present moment, as Piet Huygens sat picking at the combination of processed plankton steak and freeze-dried vegetables that constituted his meal, he was aware that the conversations on either side of him were progressing in a depressingly normal manner. To his left a couple of junior-grade engineering lieutenants were speculating on the sexual adventures which they, as Corps officers, were likely to enjoy during the stopover on Kepler III; and on his right, Lieutenant Quat, a very senior quartermaster, was holding forth to the table in general on the revolting nature of a particular type of recycled protein which was no longer used aboard Corps ships.

It required little effort on Piet's part to shut out such chatter and concentrate on his own preoccupations. During the forty-eight hours since the conclusion of the *Wangituru* operation there had been no opportunity to see Mia, but his relationship with her had been constantly in his mind. There had been ample time for his imaginative mind to return over and over again to its speculations about the possible consequences of the decision they had made. During the duty period recently completed he had found himself distracted and depressed by a combination of foreboding thoughts and a general feeling of malaise which left him operating at less than accustomed efficiency. The malaise was vaguely reminiscent of a minor virus infection, but he had a suspicion that it was more likely psychosomatic in origin. At any event, he had foregone the temptation to report its presence to Maseba, because the surgeon lieutenant had a habit of probing too deeply and too efficiently into such matters. Instead, he had dosed himself with a couple of mildly euphoric pills and carried on. Even so, he was aware that he had been saved on several occasions from making stupid mistakes in routine by the quietly efficient intervention of his P.O. orderly assistant. He would have to watch . . .

Jerking out of his train of thought he noticed that the hitherto vacant chair opposite was now occupied. Trudi Hoffman was looking at him, as though expecting a reply to some question or remark which he had not even heard. Her expression told him absolutely nothing, except that he had maybe missed out on some small talk.

"I'm sorry?" he said, enquiringly.

"I said, 'I've been expecting you,' " she replied, with a touch of flatness in her voice.

"Oh!" he said, uneasily. The assignation made in the bloody surroundings of the dissection room on the *Wangituru* had completely slipped his memory, but he could hardly tell her the truth. "I've been pretty busy," he explained. "There were a number of details to be tidied up over the processing of the stuff for the replacement banks."

Her sharp blue eyes glinted her disbelief. "I see. But you are off duty now, for a while, I believe?"

Believe . . . he guessed that she had probably made it her business to find out. "Well, yes . . ."

"Good; then I'll expect you about twenty-two thirty?" Her voice was as impersonal as a sheet of Part Two Orders. "Lieutenant (j.g.) Piet Huygens will report to Lieutenant Hoffman's cabin at 22.30 hours with phallus at the ready, prepared for sexual drill." A feeling of nausea gripped him as he pushed the hardly touched plate of food to one side.

"I'm sorry, Trudi. I'm feeling pretty beat. I thought maybe I'd catch up on some sleep. . . ." The sentence trailed away lamely as he gazed into her hard eyes.

"Or what we suffered in former times. Look at us. Total luxury! I've done an entire eighteen-month trip living on concentrates and cellulose fillers, with no-

where to take a girl except in an open dormitory—
hammocks at that. . . . No crossing ranks there—everyone could *see*." The subject of Lieutenant Quat's mono-
logue shifted smoothly back to Topic A as he addressed
himself to the table in general.

An engineering lieutenant next to him was amused.
"You mean all the crewwomen in your day had their
ranks tattooed—somewhere obvious?" There was a
burst of ready laughter from his companions.

Quat said: "It has always been my belief that the
regulation against off-duty consorting between commissioned and noncommissioned ranks is a lot of old
kluk. If they weren't sensible, well-adjusted women in
the first place, they wouldn't be in the Corps. . . ."
Quat was squarely astride his favorite hobbyhorse now,
expounding his theory of sexual democracy for the
Corps. But Piet's eyes were still held by those of Trudi.
Her face was blank and cold, but behind the mask he
sensed a growing, dangerous rage.

Then suddenly her eyes snapped away, and she was
smiling a hard, bright smile as she addressed Lieutenant Quat, who had paused momentarily for breath. "I
disagree, Phunim. Discipline could very easily go to
pieces in that way. Not immediately, of course, but
over a period of time, if rank differences were too
great, then it would be bound to suffer. After all, there
are some who think that between a chief petty officer,
for example, and a GD crewwoman the gap is already
too great; imagine, for instance, the possible consequences of such a relationship between a lieutenant and
a crewwoman, even a leading crewwoman."

"A harmless association for mutual relief," suggested
Quat, blandly.

"Ah, but *harmless* . . . there's the rub," persisted
Trudi. "Who is to tell when such an arrangement might
become something more than merely an association
providing mutual satisfaction and develop into a more

personal one? And once that happens, what price your disciplinary structure then?"

Watching the coldly attractive features of Trudi, Piet was gripped with a panic that filled his throat. Trudi was looking away, avoiding his eye—but there had to be something more than mere coincidence behind her words. She wasn't addressing him directly, but she was, in her coldly oblique manner, giving him a warning that she knew about his relationship with Mia—a warning, and a threat. The questions now must be, how much did she know? And what was she going to do about it?

". . . the medical viewpoint on such an assertion?"

Piet was jostled out of his concentration by the tag end of Lieutenant Quat's question. He stared stupidly for a moment into the beaming moon-face. "I'm sorry —I wasn't listening. What was that again?"

But before Quat had time to repeat his query, Trudi had taken the initiative. Her smile was hard as beryllium steel alloy as she looked directly across the table at Piet and said: "My dear Phunim, there's no point in asking Lieutenant Huygen's opinion on such matters. He'll merely prescribe a course of pills, and I'm sure you'd rather not take that way out of your dilemma."

Piet smiled weakly in response to the general laughter and got up out of his chair. As he hurried out of the mess he was aware of the steady gaze of Trudi's pale-blue eyes and the threat that lay behind them.

Petty Officer Herbert Dockridge was an anomaly. Officially classified as unfit for active space service because of his badly repaired leg, he had been included in the crew of *Venturer Twelve* only on the personal request of Commander Bruce. Dockridge had been his personal orderly and occasional confidant for over five years and as such Bruce apparently found him indispensable. Dockridge's official position would have been difficult to define, strictly according to regulations; he worked as Lindstrom's orderly as well as Bruce's, but over and above such duties, he kept his finger on the pulse of what was being felt aboard ship, as opposed to what was being said and being ordered. Such a position would have been an ideal one for a first-class fink, but Dockridge was nothing of that sort. He was capable of keeping his mouth shut, and he had enormous tact. In ratifying his appointment, Psyche Department had given some consideration to the fact that Doc was one of those rare and valuable people who have a natural gift for easing frictions between personalities. If officers like Bruce and Lindstrom were the controlling gears of the organization that was the crew of *Venturer Twelve,* then Dockridge was, by the same analogy, the oil that smoothed the operation of that organization. The men of the crew respected his experience and tact, and to the women, particularly the younger ones, he functioned as something of an uncle/father-confessor figure. Everyone knew him with his gorblimey voice, his terrier face and his slight limp.

He came up behind Mia as she was checking a junction box near the main elevator at eighth level. "Hello, Far Eastern. What yer doing GD electrics job for? You're radar, ain't you? Laborer's job, this."

Mia turned her head and smiled at him. "Just obliging a friend. She wanted to finish a little early."

Dockridge nodded thoughtfully. "Yes. . . . This is about the time . . ."

"Time, Doc?"

"When he starts to need she a bit more than they thought they would."

"Why's that, Doc?"

Dockridge leaned against a bulkhead and gently massaged his left leg, a characteristic gesture. "Obvious, innit? The physicists will tell you that in a ship like

this, equipped with anti-grav and inertialess drive it
don't matter to the crew if she's traveling at point ten
zeros five light, or full out. They say the crew can't
tell, and that there is no physical effect on the body.
Maybe that's so—but there's something more to a human being than a collection of flesh, bone and internal
plumbing. Travel fast enough and far enough and people begin to feel it, deep down in the psychological gut.
Call it the old terror of the unknown, the jungle feeling,
if you like, but that's the way human beings are made.
And they react to it. I know. I seen it, and I've experienced it a hundred times. So, like I said, this is
the time when she and he got off-duty periods coinci-
dental that they need each other a special kind of
hunger. Back to the womb, if you like. The old funda-
mentals that we're all built on. Of course, the young
'uns feel it especially." He scanned her pretty face with
a sharp, friendly glance. "Don't you reckon so?"

"How should I know?"

"Stone me! What a question." Dockridge shook his
head. "Warm little donah like you. Smart as paint, you
are, Mia—don't tell *me* you don't know."

"Well, yes, I suppose I do. But I've never heard it
put like that before."

"Well, there you are, the Dockridge Diagnosis.
Strictly amateur stuff, of course, but between you and
me the professionals can't do much better."

She clipped back the junction box and packed her
tool kit.

"We got three good medics," he went on, "but they
don't know everything. George Maseba, who knows
the most, admits how little he really knows, sometimes ..."

Now Mia was ready to go, but she listened to Dockridge. She found that she was listening quite hard.

"Know what Maseba said to me, once? He said 'I
wish I had the skill to rebuild myself.' I asked him
what he meant. He said that one of the troubles of his

job was that you spent so much time playing God that you began to ignore your own failings, and that because you were a doctor, other people preferred to ignore them too." He smiled at her, kindly. "You ever think that?"

Now Mia was quite intent. "You mean me, particularly?"

"Yes . . . you. You're just a little girl; at the age—and the time of voyage—to chuck down all you've got in one grand slam. I should be careful, Mia, I should, really."

"But what do you mean?"

"I wouldn't carry tales," he assured her. "Not this sort, gel, not this sort."

"But, Doc—" Now she was troubled. Clearly, he either knew, or he had guessed something.

"All right, chick. Don't upset yourself. Just think about it."

She looked into his face, and somehow, despite its strange, Western features, he reminded her of her father.

"Just remember what I said about the big dark outside. You think it *stays* outside, but it don't. It creeps into your mind, gel, because there's room for it there, still, no matter how civilized you are." He patted her cheek, and limped away.

One table in the senior officers' recreation room was permanently reserved for the chess board on which lieutenants Maseba and Helen Lindstrom played a never-ending series of games during their off-duty periods. As they walked into the room together, they saw a white card in the middle of the board.

Lindstrom picked up and read aloud from Magnus' impeccable script. "White to mate in five, I think—

and have you been teaching your bishops to *waltz?* C.M." She showed it to Maseba.

"Damn him," muttered the senior medical officer. "That's the second game he's screwed up for us." He sat down.

Lindstrom followed suit. "Shall we do as he says?" she asked.

Maseba nodded. "I guess I'm just about up to it." He put his chin on his hand and stared hard at the board. "He won't find Kepler III any chess game, I think."

"How's that?"

"Just that I've been doing a bit of homework," Maseba said. "Did you know that the population of Kepler is approximately seventy-five percent Japanese?"

Lindstrom frowned. "So?"

"Just a hunch, but there seems to be a tendency on colonial planets for racial and cultural characteristics to become more pronounced, a kind of defense mechanism, a clinging to the known patterns."

"I'm still not quite with you," admitted Lindstrom.

"No? Well, just take a look in the historical section of the library next time you've an hour or two to spare. You might start with the landing of Commodore Perry in Japan, back in the nineteenth century."

"Over three hundred years ago . . . but surely . . ."

"I'm only speculating on the lines of a general tendency," Maseba said. "But look at it this way. Kepler III has been pretty well isolated, with a majority population of Japanese for almost a hundred years, and it seems reasonable to suppose that during the time the 'Japaneseness' of the colony's culture will have become more and more pronounced."

"All right, supposing that is the case, surely it can't be a bad thing," said Lindstrom. "After all, the Japanese are a very civilized race."

"Yes, indeed, to the extent of looking upon Westerners as barbarians; an outlook with which I, as an African, must have some sympathy," Maseba replied.

"Then how will this make Magnus' task more difficult?"

"Because our friend Magnus, as we both know, is a man completely devoted to Western pragmatism, an apostle of the God of Logic," said Maseba. "The Japanese, on the other hand, despise logic and logical thinking; they prefer to rely on the intuitions of what has been called the 'Kimono Mind.' "

Lindstrom smiled. "You're exaggerating, George—you must be."

Maseba shrugged. "Maybe . . . we shall see. Now—do we play chess?"

She slipped in from the dimly lit corridor and thrust herself into his arms, kissing and receiving kisses, change and exchange until they were both slightly breathless.

At last, pulling her face away from his, she looked up at him, smiling. "Piet, love, you look cleaner than when I last saw you."

"Last? Oh, the butcher's shop. Yes." He ran a hand down the front of her zipsuit. He needed the comfort of her body much more than any talk.

She stayed his hand with gentle firmness, and stepped back from him.

"What . . . ?" He stared his bewilderment, painfully aware of his throbbing need, as she unrolled the left sleeve of her suit, right up to and past the elbow joint.

"First—this," she said, placing a finger on the slight bulge beneath the skin that indicated the presence of the contracapsule.

"Now?"

"But of course, now," she said calmly. "You have your instruments?"

"Well, yes . . ." he replied awkwardly. Desire drained out of him like air out of a pricked balloon.

"Piet, you're not having doubts at this stage, are you?" she regarded him with a sudden keenness.

He wanted to turn away, but her eyes held him. He felt as though a scalpel were being screwed into his stomach.

"Piet, love, what is it? Piet!" She moved towards him.

He looked down at her, doubt and anguish grinding in his mind, even as they had when, as a boy of eleven, he had listened in trembling alarm to the acidulous, refined arguments that took place between his mother and father when they thought he was asleep. He said: "Nobody has ever done this before, you know."

"But it has to go, Piet. You must see that. How do we get our baby, unless you remove it?"

He felt anger rise within him, and he strove to contain it. The whole thing seemed to be so easy for her, but for him it was just not that simple. "Look, this is . . . it's against all regulations, you understand?"

But she didn't. She looked at him wonderingly. "We've been over all that. We're checking out at Kepler III, aren't we? I thought it was all settled."

"Now listen, Mia . . ."

"No, you listen to me! I'm no pleasure girl, Piet. I'm not from the Ginza. I'm a worker from Haneda. I'm old enough to have had two children at least already, and another coming soon. But I didn't have them, because I hadn't met my children's father. Now I have. Isn't that right?"

He sighed, exasperated. "Oh, stop talking like an ingenuous kid! As a doctor . . . I've made certain promises . . ."

"When you didn't know the value of those promises. We said all that. And as for your doctor's promises, once upon a time they'd have said that in taking this capsule out you were doing the right thing."

"Shut up for God's sake!" he cried. "There's so much to this—the Corps point of view, the medical point of view . . . and you go on chattering as though we were the only two human beings in the entire universe, as though . . ."

"As though you loved me in the way I love you?" There were tears in her eyes, but a sudden bitter sharpness in her voice. "Love sees its own reflection, but maybe you just broke the mirror for me. Perhaps all you needed was a new bedmate with just that hint of extra piquancy because of the danger of crossing ranks, Officer Pig! In the past month I could have comforted a dozen good Eastern-born crewmen, and have been glad to do it, but no—I was a fool. I fell in love with the cold European, so much in love that I thought I could teach him what he lacked in feeling. Now I see that I can't! Well, go to your big lanky European women, then! Go and mount one or two of them— they look like horses, anyway!"

He grabbed her before she got to the door, and held her by the wrists as she struggled, avoiding an upthrust knee which would have put him out in a flash. He had never imagined her capable of such burning anger, and yet he knew that surely he himself was to blame, because he was such a stranger in the country of love.

He wanted to tell her so much, to explain, but instead he remained mute, holding onto her, keeping his eyes closed for some reason he barely understood. And soon she stopped struggling, and she spoke to him as she used to speak. "Piet . . . Piet, love. . . . Open your eyes."

He obeyed.

"Oh, Piet—you're crying. Oh love, love, were you crying because I hurt you?" Her deep affection welled up again in a warm flood, drowning anger. She made him sit down, and held him like a child, stroking his hair, letting him sob until he had no more tears.

Then she said: "Forgive me—I said such bitter things. I know you love me."

"There's nothing to forgive. I deserved it, Mia. I'm a coward; I've always been a coward. . . ." He watched as she rose, took his instrument case, and sat down beside him again. She unzipped the case, and gazed with childish wonder at the array of gleaming equipment. Then she clapped her hands.

"I know! Let's do it together. You said it was easy. What's first?"

The warmth of her love melted his fear, and he realized that he could not do less than measure up to her determination. He took up the instrument. "The freezer," he explained. "It cleans and anesthetizes, so that you won't feel the electric cutter. Are you sure you want to watch?"

And she laughed at the first touch of the freezer, and said that it tickled.

Soon the capsule was out, emptied of its estrogen solution and put back in place. When the neat incision was covered by a fast-drying plastiflesh spray he put away his instruments, and washed his hands again from habit.

Turning back to Mia he saw that she had removed her zipsuit and was lying on the bed, her exquisite, golden body completely naked.

"Now, Piet, love!" she whispered. "This time for real, with no barrier between your seed and mine."

It was not true, of course. The estrogens would remain in her bloodstream for several days until eliminated by the natural processes. But symbolically, at least, it was true.

Eager, thrilling to the promise of new-found experience, he removed his own clothes and slid into her waiting arms. Arriving there, he lay quite still, momentarily frozen by the shock of something that had never happened to him in his life before. He was utterly and completely impotent.

Although her need must have been great, Mia made absolutely nothing of his failure. She was gentle with him, holding him close, suckling him at her breast, soothing him until he slept.

And when he awoke he was a man again, and she received him with joy.

In the sickbay, Piet Huygens had just finished sterilizing the raw and bleeding arm of a huge brown crewman from Fiji who had been involved in a minor accident in number six storage hold. The crewman sat there, blinking with mild brown eyes and not feeling a thing, his mind more occupied with his inevitable pending appearance before Commander Bruce, and the tongue-lashing he would get for carelessness, than with his wound. Piet picked up the stitcher, set it for stroke, tension and width, and ran it up the numbed gash. Then, after the stitcher had tied itself off, he sealed the wound with a spray of plastiflesh.

Caiola came in with a small phone and plugged it in near Piet. "Message for you, sir—from bridge control."

Piet dismissed the crewman and moved to the phone, speaking his name.

"Huygens? This is Lieutenant Commander Lindstrom. Lieutenant Hoffman has cut the palm of her hand. I sent her off to her cabin. Could you attend, please?"

With a tight feeling in his stomach, Piet answered courteously. "Yes, ma'am."

Lindstrom had broken contact before he realized that he hadn't had the sense to ask which cabin. So Lindstrom must know that he knew which cabin. So . . .

Grabbing his kit from a rack, he called to tell Caiola where he was going, and went out to the elevator. Arriving at the cabin door he hesitated for a moment before tapping on it. This was a place he had not been for almost two months, and inside . . .

He knocked on the door, and heard her call him to come in.

She was seated on her bed, smoking one of the thin cigars she used in imitation of Lieutenant Commander Lindstrom. She wore an off-duty zipsuit and there was a clumsy plastiflesh patch on the palm of her right hand.

"Hello, Piet." Her voice was level and controlled, and he found himself thinking that she was good-looking, that she had a body which was both enjoyable and capable of enjoyment, and that life had been simpler when . . .

"Hello," he said. "Sorry to hear you hurt yourself." He sat down with his kit on his knee. "Let's have a look at it."

A spray of solvent removed the plastiflesh quickly. He probed gently at the open wound, and found that it was more of a scratch than a cut. "You must have told the commander that this was deep," he said, looking at her curiously.

"Yes." She spoke softly. "I did tell her that."

"Why? To waste the firm's time? No need to have come off duty . . ." He glanced at her zip suit. "And certainly no need to have got undressed."

"Yes! There was a need," she said sharply. She put her free hand on his shoulder, and what he had half-suspected was now confirmed. "Piet—haven't you any feeling for me now?"

He rose, awkwardly. "Look, Lieutenant Hoffman, I am on duty, you know. I'll just see to the cut and—"

"Piet!" Her voice was harsh and urgent now. "Don't you understand what you've done to me? We had a good relationship, the best. And then, suddenly, it stopped, because you didn't come to me any more. And now I find that I can't do without you. There's nobody who gives it to me the way you did . . . no one who anticipates, understands, waits and hurries, takes time and lingers, changes and repeats the way you did. Don't you understand? I feel awful—but awful!" A note of hysteria had crept into her voice, her pale-blue eyes were staring widely. "Piet, for God's sake! Give me fifteen minutes of your time, now, now!"

Her hand wrenched at the fastenings and her zipsuit fell to the floor.

He regarded her nakedness calmly. "Well, if you've been round all the male officers and there's no phallus to suit you, you'd better start on the crew."

For a moment her pale body seemed frozen with the cold shock of his words, then, with a choking noise wrenching at her throat, she lunged forward, slapping his face with the full force of her rage. "You bastard, you supercilious bastard! You—you do as I say—*now*, or I'll let Bruce know that you've been crossing ranks and taking that damned little Japanese monkey into your bunk. Now—now, damn you! Do as I say!"

The blow he gave her in return sent her spinning. He dropped his kit to give her another one, and she staggered in the opposite direction with the force of it. Moaning, she collapsed on the bed, the cold light of the fluorotubes glinting on her broad, mare's buttocks.

He said: "You open your trap, Hoffman, and I'll fix you. I'll put in a malingering report on you, and back it up with a charge of attempted sexual assault on a medical officer in the performance of his duty. That will get you a course of anaphrodisiac pills that'll fix the bite in your crotch for the rest of the voyage. You maladjusted cow! You don't just need a man; you need what you're never going to get, what you could never appreciate, even if you had it—*love!*"

He left, slamming the door behind him.

Back in sickbay, Caiola said: "Was it serious, sir?"

"No," he said, tightly. "Not at all."

Caiola regarded him curiously. "Still, best to be safe."

"Yes—safe. . . ." He turned away deliberately, to examine some plates of intestines of a GD crewman. "Looks like a minor replacement job here . . ."

But he was looking past and through the prints, back into his own mind. Despite his successful bravado of a few moments before, he could see that in the triangle of Trudi, Mia and himself, it was he and Trudi who were really alike. Trudi is me, he thought, we are male/female, two of a kind, manufactured like plug and socket, nut and bolt. But there's one difference. She is content to be that way. Me, I want to be really alive, like Mia. But can I make it?

The thought was depressing, only to be assuaged, if not cured, by Mia herself, and turns off-duty would not coincide for another sixty ship hours. Until then, there was only work.

"Get this man up here," he said harshly, to Caiola. "We'll begin the op in half an hour . . ."

"But . . ."

"What the hell, man! Let's do it—*now!*" he snarled.

Venturer Twelve sped on towards Kepler III at a speed which would have rendered her invisible to human eyes, had there been anyone to observe. Lights were brightened for "day" and dimmed for "night." Water and waste were recycled, and recycled again. Men and women worked and watched, and cleaned and controlled. They slept and pretended, as Dockridge said, that the big dark was outside, while in reality it ate a little into the normality of everyone. And Maseba, De Witt and Huygens watched this corrosion, dispensing antidotes for fear, depression and hysteria, so that all crew members remained well-adjusted and cooperative . . .

And some remembered the words of Kavanin, poet of man's impudent, star-flung adventure:

> Here we work close together, or perish
> On new lands a lifetime from home;
> All other men's skills we must cherish,
> All other men's hearts are our own.

Fresh vegetables from the Hydroponics section became more precious, each leaf a reminder that Earth still existed, beyond the unimaginable gulfs of space, each mouthful a blessed sacrament, a renewal of faith in the reality of home.

Lindstrom and Maseba had played fourteen games of chess, not counting three which spectacularly aborted because of Magnus' ability to see twelve moves ahead, and his insistence on telling them, while steadfastly refusing to participate directly in the game.

There had been one "full alarm stations," plus sealing drill, while engines took in new reactor material.

Magnus conferred with his assistant Ichiwara, and they planned the routine of the coming investigation, with special reference to Ichiwara's personal assessment of certain cultural aspects of Kepler III. Magnus, in his off-duty periods, achieved much satisfaction from his recreative activities, and gave some in return.

Medic Lieutenant Piet Huygens struck up something of a friendship with Ichiwara, and showed a considerable interest in the work of the latter, who willingly provided him with what amounted to a crash-course in Japanese philosophy and culture.

The op theater did three appendectomies, one leg fracture, replaced a crushed hand, had three agonizing shots at an optic nerve before they got it right; the Chinese crewwoman from the *Wangituru* was given a new intestine, and was tearfully overjoyed to find that with a slight skin colorant her damaged half-face could now match the other. Astonishingly, Warrant Officer Panos had to be circumcised, and he begged the medic staff to let no hint of it come to the ears of the crew. Bull that he was, he could not have stood the laughter, though he could not subdue a smile himself when Maseba said, drily: "Somebody's sure to notice, aren't they?"

Lieutenant Wiltrud Hoffman performed her duties silently and efficiently, with darkness creeping behind her eyes.

Lee Ching put an armaments storeman on a charge for losing a forty mil shell warhead, producing a wrangle with Lieutenant Quat, who claimed that this was his department, and Bruce cursed them both for pettiness, while docking the storeman a week's pay.

Far, still far ahead, lay Kepler III, where people waited in happiness, in hope, in apprehension—and some in sadness and fear—for the arrival of the ship that would decide their destiny.

And within her womb, Mia Mizuno's child grew, filling the girl with throbbing happiness—the living proof of her and Piet Huygen's love.

Give me my eyes and ears;
Let me probe deeply, let me see
The shape of passing worlds,
The smell of danger.
Let me plot the meteor shower
Progressing at barely measured speed
Across the universe,
Whence coming, where going. . . . You asking me?
Brother, it's there, that's all I know.
Never come to ask
How long it's traveled to this moment,

Or how long, into the recesses of the future,
It will travel, travel, travel,
Or turn to drifting dust in some red atmosphere
That's death to us, but spawns up things
Unguessable to earthman's sanity.
Let me talk subetheric to ships; and out to planets
Where earthman seed, precariously sown
Takes watchful root . . .

Telecoms: I. Kavanin

Shanon Kido, president of the Kepler III colony, was a round man, his sleekness carefully controlled despite his voracious appetite by lypolitic drugs to a point just below that of obesity. Seated comfortably behind his huge, uncluttered desk he stared with some severity at his Minister of Health. "It seems to me that you would be better employed in searching for an effective vaccine against this disease than in attempting to persuade me into taking such panic measures."

"Then you refuse?" It was unthinkable that one should lose face by an unseemly display of anger, but Kenji Sato was very close to doing so. There were times when Kido was so much the politician that it was almost impossible to communicate with him on the level of common humanity.

"My dear Sato—please don't press me any further," Kido said blandly. "I have it on your own authority that this Johannsen's disease is a comparatively mild virus infection which leaves its victims none the worse after a short period of discomfort. To launch a program such as you suggest would surely be giving the outbreak a greater measure of attention than it deserves. Apart from that, at this particular time such action would be decidedly unwise."

In other words, thought Sato, not politically expedient. Controlling his passion he spoke with deliberate care. "As I have explained to you already, Mr.

President, the main source of my concern is not the disease itself, but the alarming rise in the number of aborted and abnormal births, due to pregnant women becoming infected."

Kido assembled his round features into a smoothly sympathetic smile. "Kenji, don't you think that you may be allowing your own tragic experience to influence you in this? After all, the number of births is still comparatively small."

Sato was in his middle forties, about the same age as the President, but in contrast with the groomed plumpness of the other, his black hair was already flecked with gray and his bony face eroded by lines of strain. His thin body seemed to vibrate with tension as he leaned forward in his chair. "Small, but rising," he said. "As your Minister of Health you must at least accept my advice that the disease should be made a notifiable one."

"To what purpose?" Kido asked. "Until there is an effective vaccine, surely the only result of that would be to create unnecessary alarm in the minds of our people?"

"Perhaps there would be some concern," agreed Sato. "But the measure would at least produce reliable statistics. At the moment we know that the disease is on the increase, but we have no definite figures."

"And these figures—will they eradicate the disease?" Kido folded his plump hands together on the desk top. "No, Kenji. I appreciate your concern, but there are greater issues at stake. Do I need to remind you that we are approaching a supremely important phase in the history of our planet? *Venturer Twelve* will be landing within a few days, bringing the Explorations Division officer and his staff, who will investigate every aspect of our life here on Kepler III. In every other respect we are prepared for that investigation, and confident of its outcome. But if we were to take measures of the kind you advocate, indicating that there is a serious infectious disease endemic among our population, what effect do you imagine that might have on his decision?"

"Then you suggest that we deliberately conceal the facts from this investigator?"

"Conceal? My dear Sato, such a harsh word," Kido said. "We will cooperate with the investigator in every respect—but it will not be necessary to draw his attention to the existence of this minor outbreak."

"And if he finds out about it anyway?"

"Then it will be my task to explain to him the unimportance of it," Kido said. "But I do not think that this will arise. There will be a great number of other matters to occupy his energies. He will be accorded the full measure of our hospitality; all doors will be opened to him, but he will be under careful surveillance throughout his stay. For such an illustrious visitor could we offer anything less?"

"I still think you're wrong," protested Sato. "If we were completely frank with him from the outset, then there would be no need of concealment. There will be a team of Corps medics aboard the ship. With their help we could probably stamp out the outbreak in a few weeks."

"Probably," Kido said. "But we dare not take a chance on anything less than certainty. You have already told me that the normal antivirus measures are ineffectual against this strain of the disease. How can you be sure that the Corps medics would be any more successful than you have been?"

"But they have all the latest Earth techniques at their fingertips," protested Sato. "Not to mention a comprehensive bank of serums and attenuated viruses."

"Do you really imagine that they would be allowed to use those resources?" President Kido's smile stopped short on the border of being patronizing; it was the indulgent, half-pitying expression of an uncle who views with disappointment rather than anger the stupidity of a willful, not very intelligent nephew. "Kenji, my dear fellow, can you reasonably suppose that this investigating officer would forego an opportunity to deny us independence? Under the circumstances he could place the entire planet in quarantine, and defer his decision indefinitely. As a result, the Excelsior Corporation would be able to maintain its hold on us for another ten, perhaps twenty years. Is that what you want for our people, Kenji?"

For Sato, whose great-grandfather had left the squalor of overcrowded Earth almost a hundred years before to play his part in the taming of the virgin planet of Kepler III, whose grandfather had been born on that planet and labored all his life in the mines of the northern province, and whose father had been one of the first graduates of the Kepler III University Medical School, there was only one possible answer. The people of Kepler III had long since discharged their debt to the Colonization Corporation which had provided their forefathers with transportation and basic equipment; but until independence was granted, the Corporation could legally maintain the monopoly that had allowed it to take the lion's share of the planet's productivity for so long.

Kenji Sato inclined his head in a ritualistic gesture of submission. "I shall do my best to prove worthy of your trust, Mr. President," he said quietly.

Commander Bruce was stationed in the duty chair of control with Lieutenant Hoffman standing to his right. Below the command dais, duty squad number two were at their stations; Han De Witt stood at the astrogation repeater, while Yvonne Maranne patrolled behind the duty men, monitoring each screen with practiced eyes. Slightly behind Bruce, to his left, conspicuous in his immaculate pale lavender civilian suit, Charles Magnus stood watching the movements of Lieutenant Maranne with quiet appreciation.

"Estimated time of arrival thirty-six hours from now," Bruce read the figures from the bank of screens. "It'll do. We'll take up orbital station twenty-five thousand kilometers out until we're cleared for landing."

Magnus spoke. "Commander, I would prefer it if we were to take up our position over the capital city with a minimum of fuss."

Bruce swung in the chair, his lean face hardening as he did so. "What do you think you're dealing with, Mr. Magnus—a bunch of amateurs?"

Magnus was quite unmoved. "Dear me, no, commander. Had I thought that, the request would have been phrased quite differently. The point I had in mind was that, as down there on Kepler III they will have TV cameras trained and awaiting our arrival, it would be a graceful, commanding gesture if we could take no more than one shot at getting into the appropriate orbit. It would, so to speak, set the tone of the entire operation right from the outset."

Lieutenant Hoffman eyed the civilian with something close to horror. Nobody, but nobody, talked to Bruce that way on his own bridge, or anywhere else, for that matter.

Bruce said, with a fine cutting edge on his voice: "I don't know what Corps ships you've been associated with in the past, *Mister* Magnus, but in this one—" he articulated through lightly clenched teeth— "in this one, we do it right first time. Thirty-six hours from now, *Venturer Twelve* will be in a stationary orbit over the capital city of Kepler III,—and there will be, in your so nicely chosen words, 'a minimum of fuss.' "

The withering sarcasm was completely without effect on Magnus. He smiled, and let an eyebrow twitch fractionally. "My dear commander, I had expected nothing less. You won't forget my briefing meeting at eighteen hundred hours, will you?" He turned and walked away.

Bruce stared after the tall, scholarly figure, his green eyes still sparking fire. "Bloody civilian!" he growled, then swinging his chair round to its operative position he called down to Maranne. "Anything more from Earth Central on those Rim UFOs?"

Maranne's lithe body stiffened to attention as she looked upwards to the command dais. "No, sir."

Bruce grunted. "Well, keep me posted—whatever time it comes through, I want each message immediately, understand?"

"Sir," Maranne said.

Lieutenant Hoffman watched the hatchet features of her commanding officer and wondered how long it would be before the real explosion between himself and Magnus took place. Already, with the independence investigation not yet begun, Bruce was chafing at the bit, and this new rash of UFO reports wasn't helping matters. UFOs suggested Kilroys, and the past record of Tom Bruce made it pretty plain that he was determined to be in command of the ship that made that inevitable first encounter between Man and Alien.

Bruce had his problems; so had she. She shifted her weight uncomfortably from one foot to the other as she wondered yet again whether her latest move had been a wise one. With Surgeon Lieutenant Maseba on duty it could hardly fail to be an effective one.

In the medic section, they were busy. Maseba was in the middle of his duty period, which had already lasted one and a half times the normal span, and he showed no signs yet of taking ten, or even five. Maseba and Leela De Witt were busy with setting up and running tests on the blood analyzer, a piece of equipment that would feature prominently in the routine medical investigations on Kepler III, which would include a detailed checkup on a random sample of the planetary population.

The analyzer took a blood sample, removed the corpuscles, divided it into sixteen, and then proceeded to run a series of automatic tests which showed up on its screen a minute later. At that particular moment the laugh was on Maseba; the fifth column of the histogram dealing with a test run on his personal blood sample showed a significant alcohol reading.

"Must be my after-shave," Maseba said quietly. His smile spread like a cheerful plague across the features of his assistants.

Piet Huygens came in, wearing fresh whites. Maseba was glad to see him. "Piet, man, can you do the office for me?"

"Sick call?"

"Yeah. This thing—" he waved an ebony hand at the blood analyzer, around which medic and electronics techs clustered, "this thing seems to have bugs in it, like always, just at the time when we're going to need it most. Less than thirty-six hours to E.T.A., and we'd better have it working by then. Carvalho's in the office, with the list. There aren't many. The prospect of planet leave works wonders for those little ailments."

Piet walked into the duty M.O.'s room, where the sallow, white-jacketed Carvalho had already made all preparations. Sitting down at the desk, he opened the diary. He flicked over a few leaves. "Whom do we have?"

"Five four seven seven Budoglio, E. A., Crewwoman GD . . ."

"Forget the numbers, Carvalho—just tell me what?"

Carvalho became brisk. "One check on cornea—scrap of metal removed ten days ago; two healed wounds for stripping, bruised foot, suspected tonsillitis, one otitis media, and . . ."

"And what?" Piet sensed the hesitation.

Carvalho handed him the list. "This one, sir. Crewwoman ordered down for a checkup by a duty officer, twelve hours ago. Told to report on this call."

"Show me."

Carvalho handed him the chit. Piet read the name, and became quite still. Inside him, his head began to pound, and a tight knot of rage welled in his stomach. He read: "493556 Leading Crewwoman (R) Mizuno, M. E., to report for full physical check after attack of dizziness. Ordered by Lt. W. Hoffman."

Trudi! What was the bitch up to now? She had ordered Mia to report for a checkup. Well, what if Mia did have a fit of vertigo? It wasn't *likely*. She was nearly four months pregnant, but she was absolutely O.K., he had examined her himself only a couple of days before. She didn't show a scrap, although she had taken to wearing a girdle just to make sure. Could that have caused . . .?

Piet had a stylus in his hand. As he saw just what Trudi was up to, the stylus cracked and broke. She knew. Somehow she had guessed that Mia was carrying a child. Her instinct, sharpened by frustration and hate, had told her what the truth was and, using her authority, she had sent Mia down to sick call—to a sick call which, but for the bother over the setting up and testing of the blood analyzer, would surely have been taken by Maseba himself. She knew that one look at Mia would have told the senior medical officer everything, and that he would have followed the book. And if he had done that, then Mia would suffer as no human being should ever be made to suffer, in strict accordance with Corps regulations.

"Sir?"

Piet started. "Yes?"

Carvalho was regarding him curiously. "Shall we begin, sir?"

Piet stifled his boiling rage with an effort. "Oh, yes, yes of course." *Damn Trudi . . . damn her to hell. . . .*

"Same order as on the list, sir?"

Another problem. It seemed reasonable that, as Mia was supposed to have a full checkup, she should be last. On the other hand, if he was satisfied with the working of the blood analyzer in the meantime, Maseba could well take it into his head to come in and finish the sick call himself. And then there was Carvalho; the man was no fool, and it was not normal for the medical officer's orderly to leave the office when an examination was being conducted . . .

And Carvalho waited.

Piet said: "Oh, just as they come. We'll have the full-check patient last." And he strove to attend to his professional duties. The cornea had healed, the wounds cleaned easily, the bruised foot was not serious, the suspected tonsillitis was caused by heavy smoking, and the ears of the man with otitis media were swabbed and cleaned by Carvalho.

And at last there remained Crewwoman Mizuno.

"Oh, Carvalho," Piet said, assuming an ease he did not feel. "Will you go along to stores and get me half a dozen of these ampoules?" He wrote the code number down on a chit.

Carvalho took the paper and frowned. "But, sir, these . . ."

Piet's voice took on a snap. "I want them for my ready-bag, now, please!"

Carvalho went. He was hardly out of the office when Piet had the other door open, and Mia was with him, her small round face worried. He took her by the shoulders urgently.

"Now, what the hell is this about? Were you dizzy? Were you? Or what is that bitch after? Did you tell her . . . ?"

"Piet—you're hurting my arms!"

He released her. "Look—Hoffman knew that Maseba would be taking this sick call. It's only by the merest chance that I'm here. Tell me, quickly!"

"Piet—I don't understand. She couldn't know . . ."

"Then why did she send you here? Good God! Do you know what happens to a crewwoman caught growing a child?"

"I was in radar three, doing a cell check for Maranne," she said. "I remember I had just put my hand up to my forehead, maybe stood with my eyes closed for a few seconds. When I opened them again, there was Hoffman, looking at me. It was nothing, Piet, I was just a little tired. But she wouldn't accept my explanation—she just ordered me on this call."

"And what did you say to her?"

"What *could* I say? I just saluted, said 'Yes, ma'am' and left."

Piet relaxed for a moment. Mia smiled, and it made him smile too, and feel better.

She said, softly: "It won't be long, Piet love. Not long, now. They won't get us." She drew her hand down her belly and added: "Doesn't show, h'm?"

He patted her in the same place. "Like a board." He added, with an assurance that he did not feel: "Go on. I'll sign you off all clear. But stay out of Hoffman's way, if you can."

She looked at him wisely. "You, too."

He stared at her wonderingly for a moment, his fears beginning to rise again. "You think . . .?"

"No, no, Piet love. Just remember there's not long to go now, and we'll be free." She blew him a butterfly kiss, and was gone, just as Carvalho returned with the ampoules.

The rest of Piet's duty period was spent helping with the testing of the blood analyzer. Maseba could be as much a fanatic about his own gear as was Bruce over the correct running of *Venturer Twelve* as a whole. At length, duty completed, he walked the corridor and took an elevator back to his quarters.

Opening the door of his cabin, he found Trudi Hoffman waiting there. She faced him with a gleam of triumph in her ice-blue eyes, a set smile on her face.

When he trusted himself to speak at last, he said: "Get out of my cabin!"

Her smile remained, unmoved, mocking. "And if I don't want to?"

"Get out, before I break your neck," his voice was a low-pitched growl.

She examined the end of her thin cigar, then tapped a half-inch of ash onto the floor. "I don't think so, Piet. You may be good at chopping up dead bodies, but you're not really the violent type."

He was trembling now, as he stood facing her. "You bitch, you lousy, stinking bitch!"

"Lieutenant! Hardly the way for one officer to address another, surely?"

"What do you want?"

"Explanations, perhaps. . . ." She eyed him steadily. "Or . . . do you know, I'm not quite sure. There's a great deal I don't understand, and I would so like to do so."

Every muscle of his body was stretched tight, tension increased by the quiet, mocking confidence of her manner, but he held back. *If I once lay a hand on her, I'll tear her to pieces.* . . . The thought burned red in his mind.

"Your examination of Crewwoman Mizuno, for instance," Trudi continued. "Surely it was very brief for a complete physical check? It seemed quite clear to me that the girl was unwell; that was why I sent her on sick call."

"Was it?"

"But of course; what other reason could I possibly have?"

Piet hesitated. It seemed pretty clear that she was playing with him.

"And during this lightning examination, were you able to make any diagnosis, Lieutenant Huygens?" she asked.

"The girl is perfectly fit in every respect. At the time, you saw her, she was nearing the end of her duty period and was tired."

"A-one, fit for duty, then?"

"That was my report."

"But slightly pregnant, wouldn't you say? Or didn't you put that in your report?"

Panic flowed through him in a sickening flood. She knew, *of course she knew*. Doors were closing in his mind. He could only stand, pale and shaken, staring into her ice-queen face as she continued:

"You've been sleeping with her. That much is obvious. Perhaps even understandable. After all, a little variety. I shop around myself from time to time, when the mood takes me. Of course, I'm a bit conventional about the way in which I indulge my appetites. I don't cross ranks, for instance. Come to think of it, I don't get myself pregnant, either. How did that happen, by the way? Is your little monkey woman so fertile that human estrogens don't work on her? Or did you perhaps tamper with her contracapsule? After all, you are a medic, aren't you?"

"Trudi. . . ." His voice was a strangled gasp, forced through a fear-congealed throat. This woman, this cold-eyed Norse goddess, held his and Mia's lives in the palm of her hand.

"Perhaps it's some new kick, some twisted way of proving your virility?" she said, contemptuously. "A primitive like her . . . maybe she gets a charge out of feeling a half-European fetus growing in her womb. What is it—three, four months? You'll have to move soon if you're going to abort her, otherwise it could be a bit messy. But still, I suppose she's pretty hardy; back on Earth her kind drop their pups on the side of the rice field and get right back to work, I understand."

Facing the icy lash of Trudi's words Piet was still able to console himself that there was at least one thing that she didn't know. Her automatic assumption that Mia's child would eventually be aborted proved that she had not even contemplated the possibility that he and Mia might be planning to jump ship at Kepler III. So long as she didn't know that, and so long as she didn't tell what she *did* know, there was still some hope.

"What do you want from me, Trudi?"

"What did I ever want?" she said, her features softening slightly. "Our appetites matched, didn't they? Don't tell me your monkey woman gives it to you any better than I did; or maybe you've forgotten, it's been so long?"

The message in her eyes was clear now, the tone of her voice almost pleading. It was such a simple thing that she wanted; an act that they had performed together a thousand times. He had only to say the word and the danger that threatened his and Mia's plans would be removed. Trudi would have no qualms about sharing his favors with Mia, so long as he operated as an efficient satisfaction machine; she had implied as much already. And how many times could she possibly demand his cooperation during the short time that remained before the arrival at Kepler III? And Mia . . . what of Mia? Would her own attitude be so coldly reasonable?

He knew damned well that it wouldn't. Mia would rather have died a thousand deaths than submit to such a calculated rape.

Then Mia must never know.

"All right, Trudi," he said. "Remind me."

Her eyes gleamed with anticipation as she began to undress. Ship temperature, monotonously constant, demanded little clothing beneath a thin uniform. Soon she was naked, her clean body smell, a different odor from that of Mia, in his nostrils. She sat on the edge of the bed, her long, creamy European legs dangling as she stretched her arms upwards, tautening her full breasts. Placing her hands behind her head, she opened her legs and thrust towards him with demanding, urgent movements of her pelvis.

"Ride me, Piet, for God's sake! Ride me!" Her voice was a husky moan. "Make it quick and hard, and strong!"

Afterwards, when she was gone, he had a shivering fit, and was sick.

Magnus was a careful, methodical man with something of the pedagogue in his makeup. Several weeks before, the heads of sections concerned had been presented with two-centimeter-thick copies of the E.D. officer's outline plan for the independence investigation of Kepler III, with a request that they should study it in preparation. This they had done, after their various fashions, picking out the items that were particularly relevant to their own specialties, taking whatever preliminary action was necessary, and largely ignoring the rest of the closely typed pages. It was thus with some impatience that they listened for a solid hour at the beginning of Magnus's briefing session to a careful, paragraph-by-paragraph interpretation of the first fifty pages of the outline.

It was clear to Surgeon Lieutenant Maseba, who was sitting next to his commanding officer, that not the least restive member of Magnus's captive audience was Tom Bruce. Observing the increasing tension of the commander's lean body, and the increasing grimness of his hatchet face, Maseba made a private bet with himself that if Magnus's dissertation continued for just five minutes more Tom Bruce would blow his top, a rare but not unknown phenomenon which usually resulted in severe damage to the ego, and to the subsequent service career of the person who provoked it. On this occasion, however, the situation was rather out of the ordinary, inasmuch as Magnus, with his civilian rank equivalent to that of World Supreme Court judge, was clearly senior in any kind of pecking order, either civil or military, to Bruce.

The least tolerable part about the situation for Bruce, as Maseba saw it, was the fact that although he had been supplied with a detailed outline the same as the rest of the officers present, there was in that outline hardly any mention of duties assigned to him beyond a curt acknowledgment that, as commander of *Venturer Twelve,* it would be his business to house and feed the Explorations Division officer's staff as necessary during the period of investigation, and that he should maintain the ship in readiness for liftoff at such a time as the investigations should be completed. Bruce, in other words, was relegated to the terms of a combination hotelier and interstellar bus driver. Through their short acquaintance Maseba had sufficient respect for Magnus's intelligence to realize that this treatment of Bruce could not be entirely accidental; but he had not so far been able to explain to himself satisfactorily just what Magnus's purposes were in this instance. On the other hand, his experience of the E.D. officer's interventions on the chess board suggested that here also, Magnus might very well be thinking several moves ahead. He turned his attention to the tall, slightly stooping figure whose carefully cultured voice flowed on so smoothly, never once at a loss for the elegant phrase, the precise word with which to make his meaning clear.

"You are all, I'm sure, familiar with the Magarach Principle?" continued Magnus, beaming enquiringly. Then, despite a spattering of confirmatory nods from the less somnolent members of his audience, he went on to explain: "Briefly, the principle states that any colonial population must continue to grow at a certain rate in order to preserve its cultural heritage and stability. After the first seventy-five years of colonization, during which the development of a planet can be said to be in the melting pot, to coin a phrase, population growth should settle down to a steadily rising curve. If this fails to happen, and the birth rate falls below a certain percentage, then it can be predicted that the colony, as such, is no longer viable. Now, you may ask, under such circumstances, surely the situation could be remedied by the introduction of new batches of colonists fresh from Earth? However, historical precedent shows us quite clearly that this is not the case. The introduction of such 'new blood' at this stage of development, with its inevitable dangers of clash between the 'old' colonists and the 'new,' can only result in the kind of instability which may well destroy the colony completely through conflict between racial groups, even to the extent of civil war and insurrection, as in the case of Damien II, some ten years ago, when the intervention of two Space Corps ships was required to restore order, and it was eventually found necessary to declare the colony nonviable, with the consequent evacuation of the entire colonial population. I do not intend to go into detail about the manner in which the Corps handled this particular operation; suffice it to say that there were certain questions at the time, and considerable adverse comment about the use of an unnecessary measure of violence . . ."

"Rubbish!"

Maseba winced as the unmistakable bark of Commander Tom Bruce's parade-ground-trained voice broke in on the smooth tones of Magnus, and glanced at his wrist watch. Three and a half minutes flat.

Magnus, imperturbable as ever, smiled mildly in the

direction of the interruption, and said: "You had a question, commander?"

Bruce, his lean features pale with rage, green eyes flashing, rose to his feet. He said: "*Mister* Magnus—I was under the impression that this was supposed to be a briefing session, expressly for the purpose of laying out the respective duties of my officers in the Kepler III operation."

"But of course, commander."

"In that case, I don't see why we have to sit here and listen to a crash course in sociopolitical theory," Bruce said vehemently. "You can rely on the fact that my officers will perform their duties to the letter in accordance with their Corps training."

"Ah, yes, commander," Magnus said smoothly. "That is a point upon which I have no doubt whatsoever. But unfortunately the carrying out of an independence investigation is not merely a matter of orders given and orders obeyed. There will arise inevitably in the course of any such operation certain situations which are, at this stage, unpredictable. In dealing with such situations, correct decisions can only be made by those people who are fully acquainted with the underlying principles of colonial independence."

Bruce was unimpressed and unrepentant. "Good God, man! If you spend this amount of time on preliminaries, just how long do you anticipate the entire operation will take to complete?"

Magnus drew the fingers of his right hand caressingly down the taut skin of his cheek. "That, commander, is a question which I can only answer at this stage by saying: as long as necessary. Does that satisfy you?"

"It does *not!*" snapped Bruce. "How in hell can I map out any kind of voyage schedule on the basis of 'as long as necessary'? Do you expect me to sit there on Kepler III indefinitely, with the biggest, newest ship in Earth's space force taking root under me?"

All boredom was gone from the proceedings now.

The Corps officers were well acquainted with Bruce in this mood, and secure in the knowledge that, for once, his planet-busting rage was not directed against one of their number, they watched with eager interest and a touch of pride. Seated to Magnus's right, his assistant Ichiwara stared through pebble-thick glasses, his mouth hanging open with shock in the face of such open lese majesty. Next to him, an Explorations Division secretary waited, hands poised over keyboard of her stenotyper, trembling visibly.

At the focus of all attention, Magnus remained unperturbed, his voice still cool and scholarly as he replied: "My dear commander, I thought I had already made it clear that I do not intend to skimp my work or my obligations in this matter. Six months, nine, or even a year, if necessary, are not too great a price to pay in order to ensure the secure future of this planet. Earth must live by her colonies, must accept her responsibilities towards them against the day when she may need their allegiance. If you have any doubts on this score, I suggest that you examine the memories of your own experience on Minos IV and think again. Do I make myself clear?"

All eyes turned towards Bruce, anticipating a further explosion, but the commander disappointed his audience. Lean features set hard, jaw thrust forward, he stood in silence for a long moment, then without another word, he did a smart about-turn and walked out of the room.

Magnus watched him go, with no change in his bland expression. Taking full advantage of the shocked silence, he surveyed the remaining occupants of the room in a leisurely manner, then said: "Now ladies and gentlemen, to continue. . . ."

Maseba took a deep breath and settled back to his seat, his dark eyes watching Magnus with a new hint of respect. One game to Magnus—but Bruce was not the man to accept defeat gracefully; there would be a return bout.

Two hours later, the briefing session ended, Maseba hurried back through the corridors of sixth level towards medic section, his mind already full of plans for the execution of his own particular assignments during the Kepler III operation.

Even thus preoccupied, he still took time out to greet the crew members he met on the way.

"Olo, how about that burn? No pain?"

"Kekkunen, girl, I haven't forgotten you want that crooked toe straightened."

He came across a P.O. leaning against a bulkhead and massaging his left leg. "Dockridge, one of these days I'll have that leg off and start over again."

"Blimey, sir," Dockridge said. "I wish you wouldn't. It's nothing, really. . . ."

As Dockridge talked, Maseba's eyes roved ahead down the corridor, and he saw a crewwoman moving in the opposite direction from the way he himself was going.

There was something about her walk . . . something *careful* . . . something. . . . Lithe as a cat, he took off in her direction, caught up with her and tapped her on the shoulder.

"Go tell your officer I want to see you in sick bay right away."

"But, sir . . ."

"But nothing—do as I say, girl. And tell your officer to call me, if it's not convenient." He swung on his heel and hurried away.

Helen Lindstrom had been known to swear that George Maseba, at his gentlest, had a bedside manner fit to charm the very stars out of the sky. He was exerting that charm to the full now as he took the hand of the little Japanese girl who lay in Psyche Room Four. Just above the girl's head a soothing pattern of colored lights, designed to interest and caress the mind of the watcher, changed and flowed. It seemed to Maseba that the girl saw, but that the patterns had no effect. She stared blankly, her eyes wet with tears.

"Mia, you don't want to take this to heart too much, and don't think I'm a villain."

She did not answer. Tears went on welling silently from her almond eyes like pearls of sorrow.

"Mia, you know and I know that we have to stick to the regulations." He ran his hand along her left arm and felt the embedded capsule, frowned for a moment, then took his hand away. "These things don't very often fail, maybe you've just been unfortunate. But you've let it go for nearly four months. You must have known. Why didn't you come to me?"

Still she lay silent, gazing upwards, unseeing as the webs of colored light changed and moved, and her tears flowed.

"You must see, Mia, that there's only one thing we can do. It doesn't hurt, you know. A matter of less than half an hour, then a few days rest, and after that light duties for a day or two. You'll be all right."

This time she answered him. "I'm all right now," she said quietly, her seal-brown eyes looking up into his.

Hell! Maseba's bedside manner almost slipped as he realized fully, for the first time, just what he was dealing with here. This was something more than just a simple failure of a contracapsule—it was also something more than a matter of a crewwoman evading sick report.

"You want this baby?" he said.

She nodded. Her tears had ceased now, and she looked up at him with a pleading intensity.

"You know who the father is?"

Brief anger flared in her eyes. "Of course!"

"And you want the child because it's his?"

"Because I love him," she said.

"Love! Hell and damn, girl! Not here, not on a Corps ship—on my ship. Just look at the position sensibly. What kind of a mess would we be in, if all the female crew members went and got themselves pregnant, and concealed—" Maseba stopped as he had a sudden flash. What if something of that nature really had happened, a massive failure of an entire batch of contracapsules, due perhaps to the use of a quantity of incorrectly synthesized estrogen? Could be that this girl was the first of fifty, maybe sixty such cases, each—

"Is it so strange that two people in love should wish to make a baby together?" she asked, breaking in on his waking nightmare.

Despite the possible implications of the situation, looking down into her small doll face, George Maseba found himself smiling sympathetically. "Mia, my dear, don't tell me that you've never heard the old Corps line about love?"

She frowned. "About love?"

"Yes—love," he said, gently. "I've heard it attributed to Admiral Carter, Ivan Kavanin, even President Oharo, but I've a feeling that the first person who said it was just an ordinary, faceless, nameless medical officer, like me, in just this kind of situation." He quoted: " 'On board the ships of the Space Corps sex is permitted, but love is a bloody nuisance.' "

Her round features were solemn as she considered the words. "Yes, I can see that might very well be so," she said. A brief shudder passed through her small body.

"There will be other chances for you and your man," Maseba said. "I'm not going to ask you who he is. I don't want to know. But talk to him, tell him that this is the way it has to be. He'll help you more than I can. And when we get back to Earth at the end of this tour—then if you both feel the same way, come to me again, and I'll do what I can to help you both sign out of the Corps."

"Other chances . . ." she echoed his words quietly.

For a moment his black face and her golden one looked at each other and understood all that lay between them, understood the other's irrevocable point of view.

"May I go now, sir?" she asked.

He nodded. "Yes—I'll make the necessary arrangements. You'll be fitted in with the other things sickbay has to do, and we'll . . . do the job some time very soon. Now go back to your friends in your four-bunk, and carry on with your normal duties. And—here, take these." He held up a small box. "They're 'A' sedatives, mildest of the mild. They can't hurt you, and they may make you feel a little better. . . ." Still with some irrational hope that he might win from her a smile, or a cheerful word, he continued. "I'll tell you what—I'll see if we can't arrange some planet leave for you when we land on Kepler III."

"Thank you, sir," she said, and was gone.

He filled in the triplicate form, then rose from his desk and walked through the medic section to the office where De Witt and Huygens were drafting the arrangements for the detailed medical examination of a random sample of a thousand Keplerian colonists.

"Piet, I'm afraid I've got to load an extra job onto you. It's not urgent, but you ought to fit it in, say, within the next seventy-two hours."

Huygens looked up, smiling. "Sure, what is it?"

"Girl growing a baby," Maseba said, "and there's only one answer to that. I've ordered a compulsory abortion, copy of the order to the commander. Name's Mizuno, M. E. Nice kid. You fix it. All right?"

"All right, so I blew a gasket," Bruce said. "What did you expect me to do—sit there and listen to that Machiavellian bastard airing his pet theories and getting in sly digs at the Corps without doing a damned thing about it?"

"Maybe that would have been better," Helen Lindstrom said, carefully. She and Bruce were in the commander's cabin, both smoking cigars and sipping tomato juice. She knew this man so well, better than most. She realized that when he had said, back on Earth, that their former association was over, he meant it. He could turn feeling on and off like a faucet, because he was Tom Bruce. For her, it was not so easy. The fire was still there, a quiescent volcano, well-covered and under control.

His green eyes scanned her. "Stop talking like a woman, and say what you mean."

"I don't have to spell it out, do I? Magnus is big stuff to tangle with; an adverse report from him wouldn't do your record any good. Why not cooperate?"

"Cooperate? Who isn't cooperating? He'll get all the assistance he needs on the Kepler III operation, I'll see to that. But while we're on board *Venturer Twelve* he's got to understand that *I'm* in charge."

She suppressed a sigh of exasperation, looking down deliberately, studying the rim of her glass. She realized that she had gone far enough, perhaps too far . . . Bruce didn't want to talk about it any more, and that was that. He was a stubborn man, and if he got the idea that she was trying to shield him, or to influence him in any way—or, worse still, if he should begin to think that she was taking advantage of their past association . . .

"That girl Mizuno—you've seen Maseba's report?" he asked.

She nodded. "Sad business, poor kid."

He stared at her incredulously. "Sad?"

"You realize that she wants to have the child?"

He snorted. "For God's sake, Helen! What do you think we're running here, a bloody Noah's Ark? The sooner that little matter's cleared up the better, but the thing that really bugs me is the possibility that there may be others."

"We can only hope that this is an isolated case." Helen said.

"It'd better be," Bruce said sternly. "But in the meantime, I'll have a word with the girl. An accident is one thing, but to let it go on for four months without reporting the matter!"

"No woman gives up a child easily, Tom."

"No? Then I'll have more than a word," he said. "If there are other cases, the best way to make sure we catch them early is to make an example of this silly little Mizuno bitch."

"Pour encourager les autres?" murmured Helen.

He eyed her sharply. "All right—what would you suggest? Should I recommend her for a good-conduct medal, maybe?"

Her hand trembled as she put down her half-empty glass and rose to her feet. She stared down at him. "No of course not. The silly little bitch got herself pregnant, so just whip it out and stuff it into the incinerator. Then for an encore, you could call her up on a charge while she's still bleeding and give her something charitable like two weeks' cells, or do we still have floggings in the Corps?"

She strode out of the room, slamming the door behind her. Tom Bruce remained seated in silence for a whole minute, then grinding out his cigar butt in the ashtray he swore.

"And what the hell was all that about?" he demanded of the empty cabin.

Back in his own cabin after the end of his duty stretch, Piet Huygens sat on the edge of his bed, staring unseeingly at the blank gray wall opposite. There, in the metal womb of *Venturer Twelve,* despite the near presence of nearly five hundred others of his own kind, Corps people, he was conscious of a dreadful feeling of isolation such as he had never experienced before.

The direct, impersonal order to murder his own child had been a tearing aside of the golden veil of illusion; a destruction of the hazy, inspired dream that Mia had so carefully nurtured in his mind. Now with the ruins of that dream dissipated in the bleakness of space, he sat and tried to grapple with the reality of his situation, and the shadows of hitherto-suppressed doubts crept in on him like grinning specters, mocking his foolishness.

There was no consolation in the tapes Ichiwara had so gladly loaned him. They painted a picture of a civilization so strange, so alien, whose values, whose very manner of thought was completely different from those he had learned from birth. For Mia, life on Kepler III would be like walking back again into her own past; but for him he had the feeling that, whatever cosmetic changes were made in his outward appearance, he would always be a strange dog, unable to fit in with the ways of his newly-adopted pack. Mia took it for granted that he would accept and be accepted into the social setup on Kepler III, but he was far from being as confident. And yet, once he and Mia had deserted the ship, there would be no turning back, he would be irrevocably committed to spending the rest of his life among these people with their ritualistic tea ceremonies, their cherry-blossom viewing, their delicate art, and their incomprehensible brutality.

The alternative. . . . To tell Mia now that her plan was a mad, impossible one, and that it must be abandoned; to tell her that he and she were still, despite their secret rebellion, members of the Space Corps, and that they owed their loyalty and their work to that great organization; to tell her that despite all the sophistries of lovers, the oaths of allegiance they had taken were still binding.

There was no reason why they shouldn't change their minds at this stage, before any irrevocable step had been taken. Trudi was the only person who knew about their relationship, and she wouldn't talk, not now.

Trudi. He found himself thinking of her almost with fondness, remembering the times they had each surfeited the hunger of the other. With Trudi, sex had been just that, an uncomplicated satisfying of an appetite, a welcoming, unthinking oblivion. God! What would he give to be able to plunge into just that kind of oblivion now, instead of being crushed in the iron maiden of his present torment.

Because, beyond everything, deep in the soul, he knew that without setting a foot on the soil on Kepler III, the irrevocable step had already been made; it had been made at the moment, nearly four months ago, when his searching sperm had fused with the fertile egg of Mia, and their child had begun to grow. It had been pure chance that Maseba should detail him for the job of killing that child; but whether he, De Witt, or Maseba himself did the job, the result must surely be the same; with the removal of the fetus from her womb, Mia's love for him must also die. He knew that this must be so, because he himself already knew that he could never bring himself to lie with her again after such a violation, and the effect on her must surely be even deeper.

Believing himself damned from every possible angle he found that he was drawn to a positive conclusion at last. The sooner the affair was settled, the better. It could be arranged quite simply. If he gave instructions to Caiola to have Mia brought into the operating theater and anesthetized before he arrived, then she need never know who performed the abortion. Before she came to, he would be gone, and that would be an end to it.

And afterwards? Well, there would be the consolation of Trudi Hoffman's rutting, female-tigress body, with its refuge of passionate oblivion. No love. But then love was too expensive a luxury in any case; surely he had learned that much?

He rose from the bed and began to put on his duty uniform. Now was the time to act, while the resolution was fresh in his mind.

She arrived just as he was about to leave the cabin. A light tap on the door, and she was inside, her golden doll-face smiling up at him as she said: "Piet! Piet, love. . . ."

She moved forward into his arms, and as her body came close to his own, warm, like a small sun, the shadows of doubt and fear melted away and he was once more in the golden dream. Alone he had been helpless and weak, but now, with her in his arms again, he was strong again.

She giggled with pleasure as he stripped her with hands made clumsy by the urgency of his need, and purred like a cat as he picked her up in his arms and carried her to the bed.

Afterwards, warm in the afterglow of passion they lay side by side, and she said, as her hands caressed his body: "Soon, very soon now, we shall be free."

Then she slept, as peaceful as a child. And he looked down at her, ashamed of the cowardice of his solitary doubts, the fabric of their dream once more secure around him.

Magnus's choice of Joseph Ichiwara as his second in command in this particular operation was based on a number of carefully considered factors. Ichiwara had a well-deserved reputation in Explorations Division for quiet, industrious efficiency. He had a mind like a computer, capable of producing from a vast amount of accumulated knowledge precedents applicable to almost any given situation. Additionally, he performed his duties in such a self-effacing manner that no superior had ever been able to accuse him of being overly ambitious. Magnus, untainted by any similar lack of self-esteem, admired such modesty in a subordinate. But, apart from these considerations, in the matter of Kepler III, Joseph Ichiwara was possessed of one invaluable asset by the accident of his birth; he was a Japanese, with a great knowledge of the cultural and social heritage of his people. Magnus was listening in respectful silence as Ichiwara discoursed on the matter of Japanese hospitality.

"This attitude is, you will understand, not part of any deliberate effort to conceal," continued Ichiwara. "But rather a matter of politeness and protection for the welfare of the guest. It would be considered very ill-mannered to expose such an illustrious visitor to the more unwholesome aspects of our way of life. Japanese doors have no locks, but it is a point of honor that the guest should be gently guided for his own welfare. Thus, although all doors are open to him, he is normally protected by a body of devoted guides, whose business it is to ensure that those doors lead to the treasures and pleasures of Japanese life, rather than to the discovery of anything that might cause pain or discomfort to the guest."

Magnus nodded appreciatively. "In other words, my dear Joseph, it seems that if I allow myself to be feted as such a guest when we arrive at Kepler III, then it is highly unlikely that I shall be able to do the job for which I am expressly going there."

"That is so," said Ichiwara, unable to suppress a frown of disapproval at the directness of his superior's summing up, despite the fact that Magnus was only saying in his own words precisely what he himself had been implying so delicately.

"Then we must see that I am not feted, but rather treated as what I am, an official of little importance, doing a routine job of work," Magnus said.

"I hardly think the Keplerians are likely to be persuaded to take that point of view," Ichiwara pointed out. "At this most important stage of their history they will consider it necessary to indulge in a certain amount of ceremony, and in that respect they will expect, quite rightly, a certain amount of cooperation from the representatives of United Earth."

"Your point is well taken, Joseph," Magnus said thoughtfully. "But there is still the matter of the job in hand. It seems to me that the best way of approaching this problem would be to ensure that our press releases are so arranged that my own importance is minimized."

"An investigating officer of the Explorations Division must surely attract at least some attention?"

"Possibly—but if we were to provide them with an alternative celebrity, who is apparently much more worthy of their attention, then this attention could be kept to a minimun," said Magnus. "In this respect, there is surely a person aboard this ship whose past record could quite easily be glamorized to such an extent in our releases that my own meager exploits will be completely overshadowed?"

Joseph Ichiwara smiled. "I think that is entirely possible," he said.

"Then see to it, Joseph—see to it," said Magnus, with some satisfaction.

The garden was a reminder of an Earth, a Japan, that Kenji Sato had never seen, but which was nevertheless dear to him as the birthplace of old ways and customs. That afternoon he had special need of the peace and serenity of the deep green shrubs and trees, of the gentleness of the small waterfall that trickled into a mossy pool where golden fish basked near the surface. When the official ministry car dropped him at the gateway in a quiet suburb ten kilometers east of Main City, he wandered there for a few minutes before going into the house.

The large, single-storied house was made of natural, unpainted wood, sun-bleached to a silvery gray. To the right of its main entrance the *sakura*, the cherry blossom, was beginning to spread its pale pink mist over the branches of a tree which he and his wife had planted together nearly twenty-two years before, soon after the birth of their only daughter, Yoko. He wondered if soon they would be able to plant another tree.

Allowing himself the emotional indulgence of a sigh, he composed his features and walked through the open front door of the house. Inside, he removed his shoes and placed them carefully in the cupboard reserved for that purpose; then leaving the polished wood of the hallway, he walked, feeling the comforting yielding of the *tatami* floor beneath his stockinged feet, towards the room at the back of the house where his wife would be awaiting his arrival.

Tana was seated on the floor in front of the flickering television screen, the sound of which was turned down low. As he entered she rose to her feet and bowed her smiling greeting. She was a pleasant-faced woman, still slim, wearing a pink and green flowered kimono.

"Kenji, my love." Her voice was gentle and low-pitched. She gestured towards the screen. "The Earth ship is expected to land quite soon at Rokoa field. This will be a historic day."

"Historic. . . ." He moved forward and held her hands in his own for a moment, gaining strength from the contact.

Her eyes searched his lined features. "You look tired. How was it with the President?"

He shook his head. "The same. He still refuses to recognize the seriousness of the position."

"We must have patience," she said quietly.

He avoided her eyes, gazing round the ascetically beautiful room, uncluttered by the kind of Western furniture that he was forced to use during the day at his office at the Ministry and in the hospital which he personally supervised. Chairs and beds had their uses in such functional places, but this was a home which preserved the living traditions of old Japan. His attention rested for a moment on the *tokonoma* alcove with its hanging picture scroll and a small dais on which stood a flower arrangement in a single, beautifully simple pot, a long stalk of red berries and a yellow gerbera, that was all.

"Yoko?" he asked.

"She is resting, but her thoughts are troubled. Have you any news that would comfort her?"

"Perfectly normal fetal development; both the radiography specialist and Mary Osawa are agreed on that."

"Praise to the Lord Buddha," she murmured. "Go . . . go and talk with her. She has need of such reassurance."

The girl was lying on a thickly wadded *futon* by the

open window which looked out onto the garden. The swelling of her body was evident against the loosely fitting blue kimono as she raised herself on one elbow and smiled up at him.

He squatted down beside her, the fear in her brown eyes tugging at his heart as he took her small hand in his. "Yoko, my dear . . ."

"Father . . . I had a dream, and there was this creature half-human and half-dragon . . ."

"Only a dream, my child," he said, gently smiling. Repeated tests had shown Yoko's bloodstream to be completely free of the Johannsen's disease virus that had brought her first pregnancy to its tragic conclusion. Those tests and a series of X-ray examinations had indicated that there was no logical reason to suppose this birth would be anything other than normal; but the traumatic experience of having borne that first monster was still alive, seeping its poison into Yoko's thoughts. She was a sensible, intelligent girl, a statistician, who before her marriage had worked in a responsible position in the Ministry of Economic Affairs, but in the face of this obsessive fear that the creature lying within her womb might once again prove to be something less than human she had been reduced to the state of a semi-illiterate, superstitious peasant.

"The X-ray plates?"

"Show everything completely normal for this stage of development," he said.

"Father . . . you wouldn't lie to me?" She was looking at him now, her head slightly to one side. The hint of mistrust in her expression was like a dagger in his side.

"Yoko, my dear," he said wearily. "I have explained a thousand times; the first time was due to the action of the virus during your illness—but now you are not ill, and there is *no* virus."

She bowed her head. "Forgive me, *papa-san*. I am a stupid, ungrateful child."

He reached out and raised her face, his finger caressing the smooth, golden cheeks. "You are my beautiful *sakura,* and I promise on my life that no harm shall come to you. And . . . as for the dragon dream—is it not said that to dream of dragons at such a time is a good omen, indicating that your child will be a brave *samurai,* strong as a lion and gentle in the arts of peace?"

"*Papa-san,* you are so understanding." She smiled, and it was like the morning sun rising from behind a dark cloud. She held out her arms, and he helped her gently to her feet.

They walked together into the lounge where Tana was waiting. As they entered a muted fanfare burst from the television screen.

"The Earth ship is landing," Tana said, as she hurried to turn up the sound.

Sato and his womenfolk squatted on the *tatami* floor in front of the screen. This was a moment that he, they, the entire population of Kepler III had been awaiting for many long, hard years, but in the heart of Kenji Sato there was no joy, only a growing apprehension of what the next few months must bring to him with their combined burden of cooperation and concealment.

"What a great thing it is!" Yoko exclaimed in wonder. "Floating down like a feather . . . the pictures of it in space gave no real idea. It's like a complete world, all on its own. . . ."

The screen showed the crowds around Rokoa, teeming and noisy, and hugely good-humored. At a hundred meters, the descending ship came to a stop and remained there, perfectly balanced on its invisible pillar of anti-grav. Then three great doors at a hundred and twenty degrees to the circumference, set fifty meters clear of the gigantic round plug-shape of the engines, opened up, and the telescopic legs began to descend. Upon each was a box-like foot, fifteen meters by ten by four, and each foot was capable by itself of holding the mighty ship steady.

The voice of the commentator went on tirelessly, describing the scene, and interspersing relevant background material with practiced skill.

"On Earth, at this moment, *Venturer Thirteen* is halfway towards completion, but, for the time being, this is the greatest ship of the Corps fleet; and remember, viewers, it is *our* ship, protecting us, helping us. Now the great feet are down, locking immovably on the surface of the field, and we wait next for the appearance of the two telescopic lifts which form the main entrances and exits to the ship. It is hoped to arrange for a visitors' schedule, but this will necessarily be limited. It has been suggested that whatever visitors' tickets may be available should be balloted, for, and . . . ah, there goes number three camera truck forward under the ship to give you a better view of the telescopic lifts. Now the hatch doors are beginning to slide back. At any moment now, the telescopics will descend, and soon after that the first Earth visitor will step onto our planet. There is some speculation here as to who that first man will be—Mr. Magnus, the Explorations Division officer, in charge, or Commander Thomas Bruce himself, whose heroic record must be known to all of you. . . ."

Like stiff pseudopodia, the telescopics came down, and locked as they touched the surface.

"I think, perhaps, that for an occasion like this, protocol may well be on the side of the Explorations Division officer . . . ah, now the elevator lights are on . . . and a figure in uniform is emerging! It seems then that Commander Bruce is to be the first, after all. . . ."

The crowd on the field roared; and the picture zoomed dizzily as number three camera truck raced forward to get sound as well as picture of the historic first contact.

Crewman (GD) Albert Rate, of Peterborough, England, looked up in alarm. There was a bright light shining directly into his oddly round Western eyes, a microphone thrust under his nose, and someone was excitedly asking him questions in a strange accent.

"What?" said Albert. He straightened up in his stained coveralls and ran a hand through his spiky, fair hair. "Eh?" Then the waiting millions of Kepler III heard his first historic words: "Chrissake! I got a job to do, mate. Got to check the elevator footings, haven't I? If I don't, Thunderguts'll have me balls!"

The men from Earth had arrived.

Now, with the elevators down and working, *Venturer Twelve* was in business, and the to-and-fro was beginning. President Kido had arrived for a personal meeting with Magnus; Joseph Ichiwara and the members of his staff were already establishing liaison with representatives of the Kepler III government departments, with which they would be working during the investigation, the task proceeding the more smoothly because of Ichiwara's ease in dealing with members of his own race.

On tenth level, Dockridge met Mia Mizuno in a corridor. He stopped and gave her a wary smile. "Hello, kid."

"Hey," he said, "what's this I hear?"

She smiled back. "Hello, Doc."

"You hear what, Doc?"

"This baby . . ."

"Yes?"

"Accident, gel?" His kindly eyes searched her smooth face. "Long time about it, if it was."

She looked back at him calmly, feeling that if she kept quiet and let him talk, she might learn something.

"Could have finished that almost as soon as it started, couldn't you?"

"Maybe." Her voice was carefully neutral.

"Ah, I thought so. This was love, eh? Accident or not." He shook his graying head, and once again, despite his strongly European features, he reminded her of her father. "That makes it all the tougher, doesn't it?"

Members of the crew hurried past them. Voices called on intercoms, buzzers sounded, ship noises came and went, distant relays chattered, and a hum and rattle of hawsers came from open hangars on the outside skin of the ship.

"Yes, Doc. I suppose it does." She knew that the sharp eyes were trying to weigh up her attitude, her thoughts, and not entirely succeeding. It came to her that if she couldn't fool him, then she might have to rely on his liking for her.

"Orders, gel—you got to obey orders. Always did say it's tougher all round for the women. You resigned to it, then?"

"Don't I look it?"

As they looked at each other, the gritty voice of Warrant Officer Panos was heard in wrathful communication with the entire ship. "All occupants of mess thirty-seven not actually on duty, report on the double to P.O. Patel, who will give them a lesson in basic tidiness and then put them on a charge."

Dockridge said: "No, you don't look it . . . not a bit. You should be in tears, ready to claw the guts out of the medic who tries to put you to sleep. . . . What's up, gel?"

Mia inclined her dark head to one side. "What should there be? And if there were, would I tell you?"

Dockridge grimaced. "Sometimes it helps to talk—strictly off-the-record. I ought to know—that's my specialty; listening. I'm old for crew. I seen 'em come and go. You name it, I've seen it, or been through it. And what I say in your case is this—if a gel starts a baby and keeps it growing for four months until she's found out, then she must *want it*. And if she wants it, then she ought to keep it, because God knows there's little enough of that kind of love left in the universe, and maybe there never was enough to go round."

Two sweating crewmen scrambled by, heading for the nearest elevator. "I thought *you* stayed behind to tidy up!" Then they were gone.

"Mia," Dockridge said. "You, the young ones like you, are like daughters to me. I suppose I'm getting on, a sentimental old fool, but there it is. . . ."

She looked up into his gnarled features, understanding his sincerity and loving him for it. But there was nothing he could do for her. Even his indulgence would fade quickly if he knew the real truth of what she had planned—and with whom she planned to do it.

She smiled, her natural warmth reaching out to him. "No, Doc—you're not foolish, or sentimental, you're just human, and we appreciate it . . . all of us."

"But no dice this time, eh?" he said, patting her on the cheek. "Okay . . . have it your way, gel. But remember, if you need a shoulder to weep on, or just a friend to talk to, the door's always open."

"I know it is, Doc . . . and thanks."

He walked away, and for a moment she followed his limping stride, the smile lingering on her face. Then she looked down at her watch. Timing was important. She had diligently compared regular duty schedules with extra and deputy ones, and *this* was the time. She took an elevator up to officers' quarters.

She paused outside the door, aware of the pounding of her heart. If she was wrong, she could be throwing away her chances altogether by coming here. But she couldn't be wrong, she mustn't be wrong—so much depended on her being right.

She knocked on the door.

"Come in," called the familiar voice.

Mia entered, shut the door, and saluted. Standing smartly at attention, her face was calm, expressionless, that of a model Corpswoman.

Trudi Hoffman, just showered and changed into number twos, stared at the girl, a crease of disbelief and suspicion forming between the red-gold brows.

"Well?"

"Permission to speak, ma'am."

"Granted. And stand easy. What do you want?"

Mia took a deep breath. This was it. She had decided that directness only was the plan. No hedging, nothing. Just straight out. And the success of the plan depended completely on the correctness of her assessment of Hoffman's temperament—the assumption that, despite her all-Corps exterior, inside Trudi Hoffman still thought and felt like a woman. . . .

"I want—ma'am—the chance to walk out of your life."

Trudi Hoffman came close to Mia, topping her by more than half a head. The icy-blue eyes looked down into the seal-brown ones. "Crewwoman, I didn't know that you were even in my life—but go on."

"I want my baby," Mia said. "But if I stay here aboard *Venturer Twelve* I shall lose it."

"That figures . . . I understand there's a Comp. Ab. order in existence already," said the lieutenant. "So what do you want from me?"

"A pass to get off the ship. I would be among my own people on Kepler III, once off Rokoa field I could disappear—"

"Desertion . . ." Trudi's eyes narrowed.

"Call it that, if you like. All I'm interested in is having my baby. And . . . he won't help me." No names —just the implication that she was no longer interested in Piet; that with her gone, Trudi Hoffman would have a clear field with no rivalry for his favors.

Trudi backed off and lit a cigar in a leisurely manner. "Why in hell should I do that for you?" she said coldly. "He'll lay me any time I tell him to, he has already—or hasn't he told you?"

The cold words seeped into her mind like icy water and Mia knew without doubt that they were true. Piet . . . Piet and this great blonde mare! He'd done it to shield her, to protect her, but the thought was so revolting that she was filled with nausea. What kind of a woman was this, that she could force a man to serve her in such a manner?

"No, he hasn't told me, because I haven't seen him, because I don't want to," she said, lying desperately. "All I want now is to get away and have my baby."

"Then, if it's over, why do you imagine that I would want to help you?" Trudi said. "Even if we were rivals in a sense once, we're not now, are we?"

Mia was lent cunning by her need. "Because I could talk. Only you and I know who the father of my child is, but if I were to go to Commander Bruce and tell him everything, tell him how Piet removed the contracapsule from my arm, how we deliberately made this baby together. . . ." It was a desperate, untrue bluff; but a woman like Trudi Hoffman in similar circumstances would have the venom, the ruthlessness to do such a thing, to bring about the complete ruin of the man she loved; to see him stripped of rank and dishonorably discharged from the Corps, as he must be for such crime against sacrosanct regulations.

"You dirty, conniving little cow!" said Trudi Hoffman, with some satisfaction. "I really believe you would." She moved towards a drawer and took out a pad of forms.

She filled one in quickly, then passed it over.

Mia glanced down at the precious, pale green slip of paper. The signature at the bottom said: *Y. Maranne. Lt.*

"Thank you . . . ma'am."

Trudi Hoffman's mouth twisted. "Get the hell out of here, you little whore."

Mia Mizuno, wearing a plain dark blue off-duty zipper suit with no insignia, and carrying a small overnight bag, stood waiting in the warm darkness of the mono-station at Shamari, two stops from Rokoa field. She had not realized that here on Kepler III it was the time of the *sakura*. The station platform was festive; its lamps were made in the old six-windowed style, their lights shining through panes of pink and pale green plastic, and tied to the top of each was a branch of artificial cherry blossoms. As she got off the train it was like stepping back into old Japan, a homecoming to the planet that lay many light years away across the wastes of space. The people who moved about the station, dressed in gay, bright colors, were her people, and their voices as they chattered together, sometimes in Japanese, sometimes English, were those of friends.

Looking to the east, away from the city, she could see the great, illuminated dome of *Venturer Twelve*, towering above Rokoa field; but that world was already far away. She wondered if the crewwoman on duty at the top of the down elevator had thought anything about the pass; she had clearly been envious of the fact that Mia had been granted planet leave so quickly after arrival. There would be no such questioning of Piet—as an officer. . . . She passed her hand over her stomach in response to a sudden qualm. Of course he would come . . . why shouldn't he? Had it not been arranged between them?

There was a mono every five minutes. Five minutes. . . . She looked down at the illuminated clock to the right of her, beyond the *bento* stall, and then down at her watch, and realized that they were different. The watch was made for Earth, for ship time. Here on Kepler III, with its twenty-eight-hour day, the watch would not do. It was a curiosity, and at the same time a liability, indicating her origin. Even though it was a gift from her beloved elder sister, she did not dare take the chance of keeping it.

Slipping the watch from her wrist, she glanced at it for a moment with regret, then, with symbolic firmness, she dropped it to the concrete of the platform and ground the face beneath her heel.

A succession of westbound trains came and went, and still she waited. The crowds were thinner now, and she was gradually feeling more and more alone. She looked back again towards the ship, praying that he might come soon. All she had was the clothes she stood up in, and in her small bag, the papers with the family tree carefully inscribed, and her gift for the head of the Kepler III branch, a small, exquisitely dressed Hakata doll. Such dolls had been made for over five hundred years in the old port city of Fukuoka on the island of Kyushu, but surely none had before traveled so far to find a home. In the pocket of her zipper suit she had notes totaling about sixty United Earth credits—each credit worth something like one and a half Kepler III credits—enough to keep her in food and somewhere to sleep for about a week, according to what information she had been able to glean so far. Piet, when he arrived, would probably have slightly more, but even so they could hardly be independent for very long. Clearly everything hinged on finding the family before the money ran out.

When he arrived . . . . Just as a tiny fear began to nudge her, another train glided smoothly into the station. She watched as the doors hissed open, and Piet stepped out onto the platform, outrageously tall among the other alighting passengers. She felt as though her heart would burst with its sudden weight of relief and happiness.

"Piet, love, Piet!"

She was fast in his arms, and this whole new world was suddenly perfect.

The mono on which he had arrived left, and the crowd dwindled. She peered up at him, searching his face in the patchwork glow of the lanterns.

"Your hair—did you dye it?"

"Not all—just what shows under here, and at the sides," he said, touching his cap. "And a bit of pencil on my eyebrows."

She smiled. "I can see *that*—you look like a *Kabuki* lion dancer."

He grimaced. "Thank you very much; is that bad?"

"It'll do, for the time being, and under these lights," she said, reassuringly. "In the morning I'll get some cold-water dye for your hair, and tone down the eyebrows."

They walked along the platform towards the shelter near its end. There, in false but welcome security, they kissed deeply, holding each other close.

"We're staying here all night?" he asked, at length.

She nodded. "I thought that would be best—then we could take the first workers' train in the morning into Main City. All right?"

"Yes—I suppose so. The question is, when will they miss us?"

"Well, I'm not due on duty until oh eight hundred tomorrow morning—how about you?"

"That's the trouble—if there should happen to be any kind of emergency, I could be called at any time," Piet said.

"There won't *be* any emergency," she insisted. "Stop worrying yourself, Piet. We've made it—we're away!"

But he was still frowning. "I wonder how they'll go about it? Bruce certainly wouldn't fancy getting in touch with the local police right away—the Corps image and all that stuff. I think that first he'll try to find us through his own efforts, maybe sending out a squad to search . . ."

"A squad, to search a whole planet?" She giggled. "That sounds a pretty tough assignment, even for the Space Corps."

"Be serious!" he said, sharply. "This isn't some girlish prank; we're gambling both of our lives, our futures, here . . ."

"Not just *both*," she said, quietly, touching her stomach. "All *three* of our lives."

"Of course—three of us," he said, suddenly happier.

She looked up at him. The dim light of the shelter deeply etched shadowed lines of worry on his face, and she found herself wondering whether he was already regretting the irrevocable step they had taken. Everything had gone according to plan, so far, but somehow there was not the joy of freedom she had expected. Before he had come there had been hints of that joy, the cherry blossom on the lanterns, the sound of Japanese voices . . . but then, for him, such things did not speak of home; he was still a stranger here. She felt a sudden, protective wave of tenderness towards him. For the time being, at least, she would have not just one child to care for, but two, and he must be humored.

He looked at her with widening eyes as she rose to her feet. "What is it?"

"Wait here," she said, smiling her reassurance. "I will get us some food, and something to drink. Then you will feel better."

He sat, awkwardly hunched forward, watching her go, stifling the impulse to call her back. Without her he would be so completely alone, here on this strange planet, among these strange people. . . . But then, what had he expected? He was tired, and hungry . . . suddenly very tired. Placing his zipper bag as a pillow, he stretched himself out on the bench.

"Citizen." It was a man's voice. "Citizen!"

He jerked out of his doze. A figure was silhouetted against the checkered light of the lantern. A peaked cap, the gleam of a uniform button. It was a cop.

Panic hit Piet in the middle of his stomach, and seemed to freeze him.

"You all right, citizen?" the policeman's voice sharpened.

He swung his legs off the bench and stared upwards, blinking. "Sure, I'm fine. Just tired." His voice, making a meal of every vowel sound, was a deliberate imitation of the accent he had heard coming up in the mono.

"Working late?"

Piet yawned, his heart pounding. "Or early. Six television repairs in a row, current surge. Some people can't even change a fuse." It was a wild improvisation, the first thing that came into his head, but it seemed to satisfy the cop.

"Don't have to tell me that," he said, with a flash of white teeth. "Get that kind of thing all the time in my job, helping people too stupid—or too idle—to help themselves. Still, it's a steady living. You on your own?" The question, policemanlike, was tacked onto the end of the casual chatter.

"No. My wife has just gone along the platform for some food."

"The *bento* stall? Well I hope she doesn't buy any of their *tempura*—that fish is in and out of the freezer too many times for my liking." He glanced at his watch. "Twenty-seven-thirty; I'd better be getting along. Goodnight."

Piet said goodnight, and watched the cop go. He saw him say a word to Mia as she passed him, and then carry on down the platform, a little brown man, in a pale uniform, walking with the slight swagger that would brand him as a cop anywhere in the universe.

Mia came into the shelter, and deposited two card-board boxes and a small stone bottle on the bench.

"You had a visitor."

"God! I thought he was going to ask to see my papers," Piet said.

"But he didn't, and everything is all right—and now it's time for supper," she said, laughing. Squatting on the floor in front of the bench, she opened the bottle and poured sake into two small paper cups.

"Here's to our new home," she said, handing him one of the cups.

Piet sipped the drink. It was mild and sweet, not unlike sherry, and with a pleasant aftertaste.

"You like?" She smiled up at him.

"I like fine," he said, draining the cup.

"And now for food," she said, opening up the card-board boxes. One was filled to the brim with plain, boiled rice. The other contained a mosaic of carefully arranged tidbits, the nature of which she explained to him in detail. There were two pieces of broiled fish, some slices of fiercely red sausage, a tidy knot of sea-weed, pickled roots of vegetables, some bright pink shrimps, and a miniature plastic bottle of soy sauce. Unwrapping one pair of *Hashi,* featherweight wooden eating sticks no longer than a pencil, she began to instruct him in their use.

He was clumsy at first, and they both laughed at his efforts, but somehow he managed to get a fair proportion of the food into his mouth. He found that, despite his early misgivings, it was surprisingly tasty, and certainly superior to the greater proportion of ship's meals aboard *Venturer Twelve.*

Afterwards, when the food was gone, they sat close together and drank the rest of the sake. Piet was feeling much more relaxed now, the knotted feeling in his stomach gone, a warm glow permeating his body from the deceptively sweet wine.

Placing the remains of the *bento* boxes in a litter

receptacle outside, Mia returned and snuggled up close to him on the bench. "The first train is at five-thirty," she said. "We'll get off at the Honshi Gardens stop, then I'll buy some dye when the shops are open, and you can use it in the men's room. After that, looking like real Keplerians, we'll go along to the public archives building—it isn't very far away."

"Archives?"

"To look up my relatives."

"You really think you'll be able to find them?"

"Piet, love, of course. The people here haven't forgotten their links with Earth." She cuddled closer to him.

The sun was well up in a cloudless sky when they stepped out onto the gaily decorated platform of the Honshi Gardens station. Piet, according to plan, bought a newspaper, and sat on the first seat inside the vermilion-painted *torii* gateway, hiding himself behind the sheets. He felt more relaxed now, but still far from comfortable. From behind the newspaper he surveyed the passers-by. The gardens blazed with flowers, many of them in strange color combinations which he had never seen on Earth, and the avenue was lined by cherry trees covered in delicate pink blossom. Gradually the light, warm breeze and the sunlight lulled him to sleep.

He awoke with a start to find Mia standing beside him. "Hey, sleepy-head." She thrust the paper-wrapped bottle into his hand. "The toilet's over there."

Dyeing his hair was a messy job, but finally he was satisfied. He rejoined Mia, who pronounced herself pleased with the transformation, and they strolled out of the gardens in the direction of Sol Square. The city streets were already busy with traffic, and the sun was beating down with a fierce, dry heat. They crossed the one-way traffic circuit of the square, scrupulously observing pedestrian rules; large notices warned them that they could be fined on the spot for infringements.

Mounting the white stone steps of the Planetary Museum and Archives, they were glad of the cool shades of the pillared entrance.

"Oh, look!" Mia stopped to look at the large panels of pictures and print around the entrance hall. "Who's Who in the Independence Negotiations." There were pictures of President Kido, of Charles Magnus, of the various governmental ministers, and one, in heroic stance, of Commander Tom Bruce, the green eyes staring penetratingly out at the onlooker.

Piet said, nervously, "Let's go, shall we? Find your family and get out of here."

Mia showed no sign of even noticing his unease. Bright as a bird, she led him on through the echoing corridors of the archive building, until at last they arrived at the office of the custodian. A wrinkled brown ancient with a white beard, he welcomed them with a bow and took note of Mia's request. Then he guided them to the subsection of files marked MIZ, and with another bow, left them to it.

Piet stood beside her as she leafed through sheet after sheet. In here it was still and cool, and the thronging traffic of the city outside seemed miles away.

Mia said: "One thing makes it easy. We've lived in Haneda for over a hundred years, so tracing other families won't be difficult. . . ."

He peered over her shoulder, but much of the writing was in ideographic script, so he lost interest in the papers and, fretting over the time slipping by, he walked to the window and looked down towards the square. The smoothly running electric buses had a curiously old-fashioned look, and the pedestrians in their brightly colored clothes were like figures in an old tapestry, remote. . . . As he stared, the strangeness of it all pushed his thoughts back into the regions of the familiar, the life he had left behind.

Back on *Venturer Twelve,* had his absence been noted yet? Was George Maseba even now demanding to know what had happened to his assistant? And Bruce . . . that ruthless crag of a man. He shuddered slightly. If he—

Suddenly Mia was at his elbow, her hand touching his sleeve. He looked down at her, and saw that every feature of her face seemed to have gone round with wonder.

"Piet . . . Piet, I've found them."

He exhaled air with sharp relief. "Good! I was beginning to think you'd been too optimistic. Do you have the address? Can we go there now?"

"I'm . . . I'm not sure—"

He stared at her. "But we can't just hang around the city. Any time now there's sure to be an alarm put out for us—there'll be our faces, descriptions on the local television network. Where do your relatives live?"

"Ten kilometers east of the city at a place called Tamah. But I . . . ." She stared at him, the small muscles at the corner of her mouth twitching.

"Mia! What's the matter?"

"The head of the Kepler branch of the family is a man named Kenji Sato—Doctor Kenji Sato," she said.

"Well, there's a hell of a coincidence!" he exclaimed. "So is that bad? Looks like your Doc Sato's got another medic in the family."

"You don't understand," she said, in a small voice. "Kenji Sato is not only a doctor—he's also the Minister of Health for Kepler III."

"My dear Commander Bruce, don't think I'm insensitive of your feelings in the matter," said Charles Magnus. "But you will be doing myself—and United Earth—a not inconsiderable service if you cooperate. You must realize that colonial peoples such as those on Kepler III cling hard to their associations with Earth, and it is in our interest that they should do so."

Seated at the desk in his standby room, Tom Bruce scowled down at the sheaf of foolscap sheets that the Explorations Division officer had just handed to him. The first sheet was headed: SCHEDULE OF SOCIAL ENGAGEMENTS—COMMANDER BRUCE. On the second and subsequent ten sheets, planned in precise detail, was a schedule of the appearances to be made by Bruce at public occasions on Kepler III during the next month. These occasions included everything from private banquets with the mayor and corporation of all ten major cities, to the addressing of a ten-thousand-strong rally of schoolchildren in the Kyoto stadium of Main City. Far from kicking his heels in enforced idleness, if he accepted this schedule, it was evident that Tom Bruce would work even harder during his stay on Kepler III than when commanding the ship in space; *much harder,* because for a man of his temperament, who had never cultivated the ability to suffer fools gladly, and who had always prided himself on his direct, no-nonsense approach to each problem that presented itself, the prospect of so much public speech-making and polite conversation with Keplerian dignitaries would be like entering blindfold into an area sown with land mines.

"Hell, Magnus! If you wanted this kind of public relations performer, you should have got yourself one of the pretty boys of the Corps, like Mariano, or Van

Eps. You know darned well the kind of reputation I've got."

"For speaking your mind, for complete, fearless honesty?" Magnus said, the shadow of a smile on his lean features. "My dear fellow, I know you by more than repute, and I've got the scars to prove it. But if you care to spend a little time scanning the local television channels and the Keplerian press you will see that your name, as commander of the Corps' largest and most impressive ship, coupled with your distinguished record, has made you the natural focus of attention during our stay here. As such, it is quite understandable that the people of the colony should request, even demand, the opportunity of meeting you on every possible occasion. There have already been two peak-hour documentaries—one devoted to yourself and *Venturer Twelve,* and the other concerned with your work as head of System Patrol, before you took over this command."

Bruce frowned. "Where did they get the material for such a coverage?"

"Naturally there have been releases on all aspects of the expedition by my PR department," Magnus said. "Films and tapes were provided as a matter of routine."

"But why pick me for such a build-up? After all, as you've pointed out before, what happens on Kepler III is mainly your show."

"Commander, you are far too modest," Magnus said. "Your record, without any embellishment, has been sufficient to draw attention to you. The releases on myself were equally detailed, but despite my acknowledged importance in the matter of this independence investigation, you must realize that I am a comparatively colorless figure, an obscure civilian legal expert with a routine job to do. You, on the other hand, immediately appealed to their inherent sense of *panache.* If I recall correctly, the headline of a recent page article in the Main City *Times* was: BRUCE—THE SAMURAI OF THE STARS."

Tom Bruce winced visibly. It occurred to him that he was being railroaded into accepting the role of some kind of figurehead, an image on which the greater part of the Keplerian attention would be focused, while Magnus, in his own quiet way, got on with the independence investigation unhampered by too much limelight. His military training made him well aware of the value of diversionary attack in certain operations, but the acceptance of such a secondary role did not sit easily; especially so, because he had an idea that in some covert manner Charles Magnus was laughing at him.

"Well, as you've already made these arrangements, I suppose there's not much I can do about it," he said ungraciously. "But I warn you, Magnus . . ."

He broke off as there was a tap on the door and Helen Lindstrom entered, accompanied by Lieutenant Lee Ching, who was wearing duty blues with a police armband.

Lindstrom and Lee Ching saluted smartly, and Lindstrom said: "Sorry to interrupt, sir, but a matter of some urgency has just come up."

"All right—what is it?" Bruce said.

In answer, Lindstrom produced a small transparent envelope. Tipping its contents, tiny pieces of metallic wreckage, into her palm, she showed them to Bruce. They appeared to be the remains of a wrist watch.

"Well?" Bruce demanded.

"These were picked up by a sweeper on Shamari mono station early this morning," she said. "He was going to throw them in the trash can when he noticed the numerals and realized that what he had found was an artifact of Earth origin, rather than Keplerian. He handed it to the station super, who took it to the police, and they delivered it here a few minutes ago."

"So someone on Kepler III destroyed an Earth-type wrist watch," Bruce said heavily. "I fail to see . . ."

"But that's not all, sir. According to her section head, Leading Crewwoman Mizuno failed to report for duty at oh eight hundred hours this morning, and further enquiries revealed that she had not been seen by any of her bunk-mates during the past twelve hours."

"Mizuno . . . isn't that your pregnant crewwoman?" inquired Magnus.

Bruce ignored the query. "The stupid little bitch! You mean she's gone adrift?"

"Looks very much like it, sir," Lindstrom said. "She's certainly nowhere aboard the ship."

"Damn and blast!" Bruce snapped. "Not twenty-four hours down on a colonial planet, and one A.W.O.L. already."

"Her motive is pretty clear," said Lindstrom. "She'd take any chance to save her baby."

Bruce glowered up at his second in command. "All right, Lindstrom—you can save the motivational analysis for the court martial. Assuming this is Mizuno's watch, you at least have some kind of lead. What action is being taken to trace her?"

"None at the moment, sir," said Lindstrom. "I considered it better to consult you first."

"Goddam it, woman! Can't you handle a simple case of A.W.O.L. without detailed instructions? Get onto the local police right away, and . . ."

"No, commander!" Magnus spoke with quiet but incisive firmness. "That would be very unwise at this stage—and most probably of little use."

"You mean I should let her go, just like that?" Bruce said. "Mr. Magnus, we don't do things that way in the Corps."

"I quite appreciate that in the normal course of events a deserter can expect immediate and possibly rough justice," Magnus said. "But here, I'm afraid, we are dealing with a rather special case."

"*We?*"

"Yes, *we*, commander. If the girl is A.W.O.L. on

Kepler III, as seems likely, then there are a number of factors which must be considered before any action at all is taken. In the first place, as I understand it, she is Japanese—an origin which she shares with some ninety percent of the population of the planet. She is no doubt aware of this, and is relying on the fact that once she is out of uniform it will be extremely difficult to distinguish her from a native Keplerian."

"There must be some way of tracing her. She will have no civilian identity papers, for one thing," Bruce pointed out. "If the local police put out a dragnet . . ."

"For one little Japanese girl, on a planet with a population of a million?"

"It could be done, if they cooperate."

"If they cooperate—there's the point," Magnus said, with a touch of grimness. "But I would remind you that a colonial planet of this kind is not run with the rigid efficiency of a Corps space ship, commander. Apart from that, there is the public relations aspect to be considered."

"Public relations? What the hell are you talking about? This is a domestic matter—the girl is an enlisted member of the Space Corps."

"As far as we are concerned, that is true," agreed Magnus. "But look at the situation from the Keplerian point of view for a moment. Their instinctive sympathies must inevitably lie with Mia Mizuno. She may have sinned against Space Corps regulations. but if we tried to instigate a full-scale manhunt to find her, we would be making a bad mistake. Such action could only succeed in creating an unfavorable image of the Corps as a ruthless, inhuman machine, dominated by persons of Western extraction, determined to persecute an individual who is by birth one of their own race. The fact that she is, in addition to everything else, pregnant . . ."

"I think Mr. Magnus is right, sir," Helen Lindstrom said. "Assume that we were to demand the cooperation of the local police, and they did manage to find her. What earthly use is this girl going to be to us in the future? Bring her back to the ship, and perform a compulsory abortion, and I guarantee that she'll spend the rest of this duty tour under psychiatric treatment, followed by immediate discharge when we return to Earth. She can only be a liability, so why not let her go now and forget about her?"

"Forget about her?" Bruce glared up at his second in command. "Goddammit, Lindstrom! You know as well as I do that Corps *never* forgets, particularly in matters of discipline."

"Then," said Magnus, calmly, "I think it is time that the Corps learned to temper its rigid attitude. I don't want to have to pull rank on you, Bruce, but in this instance, I must request that you comply with my recommendation to drop the matter of Mia Mizuno."

Bruce looked at the Explorations Division officer long and hard. Several times in the past he had wittingly jeopardized his career on points of principle and suffered for it. But this time, even if he stuck to his guns and insisted on having Mia Mizuno dragged back to *Venturer Twelve,* what was there to be gained?

"All right, Mr. Magnus," he said. "I'll accept your recommendation. But I shall require you to tape a full statement for the record."

"Gladly, commander," Magnus said, smiling.

Tom Bruce rose to his feet, pulling his shoulders back with conscious effort. There was a time to stand firm, and a time to retreat, he told himself. But at the back of his mind an unease was stirring. Was he, he wondered, getting old, too old for the job?

Dr. Kenji Sato had spent most of the morning in his office at the Ministry of Health poring over the draft of medical procedure which had been received from the office of the United Earth Explorations Division officer. He was a worried man. One of the major requirements of the procedure was a detailed medical examination by the Corps medical section of a random sample of the colonial population. This was a routine measure designed to ensure, among other things, that after a hundred years on an alien planet no major defects had developed in the genetic structure of the colonists through radiation and other factors. Such a requirement was logical, in keeping with the Magarach Principle, which stated quite clearly that to be viable, the first essential was that a planetary population must be capable of breeding true.

Sato had no doubts on that score. Apart from the abnormal births traceable to the cause of pregnant women being infected with Johannsen's disease, there had been no sign of any genetic mutation in three generations. But, knowing the efficient methods of the Corps in such matters, there was little possibility that the medics would fail to detect the signs of Johannsen's disease that inevitably would be present in the bloodstream of a significant proportion of any random sample. And once the virus was discovered, there would be questions.

If only President Kido had acceded to his constant urgings to make a frank statement about the incidence of the disease, which was, after all, not a killer, then it still seemed to Sato that the Corps medics would automatically throw in their considerable resources to help in the eradication of Johannsen's disease. But Kido, because of his conviction that the investigating officer would use the presence of the disease as an excuse for delaying independence, would not be persuaded. And so a course of concealment had to be followed—a lie of omission compounded by another lie of a more positive nature; the responsibility for this falsification placed squarely on the shoulders of Sato, a burden which he could not shirk, because of his own loyalty to the planet of his birth.

The manner in which this lie would have to be presented to the investigating team was already clear in his mind, but there was very little time in which to act, and there would have to be a great deal of preparatory work beforehand by skilled staff, of whom he had all too few.

There was a tap on the door, and he looked up, his face brightening slightly as Mary Osawa entered the office. Mary, a stockily built woman in her late thirties, was in charge of the Fuji hospital on the eastern side of the city. Her specialty was virology, and it was she who had been responsible for the isolation and identification of the Johannsen's disease virus. At the moment, she and her assistants were working day and night in the task of developing an effective serum against the disease.

"Thank you for coming, Mary," he said, motioning her to a chair. "How is the work progressing?"

"Slowly, but there are hopeful signs," she said, her body settling itself into a slump of exhaustion as she seated herself.

"The *bhuku?*" Sato asked. *Bhukus* were a rabbit-like species of animal native to Kepler III, which had proved useful in the role of experimental subjects in the past.

"Three of the control batch have developed Johannsen's," she said.

"And those who have been given the test serum?"

"No symptoms so far, but we must wait and see how long the apparent immunity lasts."

Wait and see—it was the constant reply, but the only sensible one. Sato rebuked himself for still retaining the vain hope for a miracle. There was to be no easy way. Even if the serum did prove effective in these experimental animals, that was still only the first stage of the operation. It would then be necessary to carry out exhaustive tests to find out if it had the same effects on human subjects. And beyond that, supposing the human tests were successful, then there would still remain the problem of cultivating and purifying sufficiently large quantities of the serum to give immunization shots to the entire population of the planet. Mary Osawa's laboratory was just not geared for such a production program, either in the matter of trained virologists, or in necessary equipment.

"Kenji, if you could speak to the President again . . ."

"That is out of the question," Sato said, cutting in on her sharply. "He has made it quite clear that he has no intention of changing his attitude. I have argued and pleaded, but he stands firm. Independence is, and must remain, the prime consideration."

"And meanwhile, those of our women who are unfortunate enough to be infected must go on bearing these monstrous children?"

"It is a price that must be paid."

She looked at him, a hint of pity in her dark eyes. "You, with your experience, can say that?"

"What *else* can I say?" he said, spreading his hands outwards on the desk top in a gesture of helplessness. "I am hoping that when Yoko's second child arrives, the effects of that disaster will be washed from her mind. It will be a new beginning."

Mary Osawa said: "I was talking to Yamaguchi on the vidphone earlier this morning. Two more cases were delivered to him last week. He and his workers are devoted to their task, but even their dedication cannot sustain them indefinitely, when there is no hope. Two cases this week, perhaps three next, and so on, until we are able to stamp out the disease. How long that will be we cannot tell at this stage. Perhaps it would be better if we were to euthanize the viable ones at birth."

"No! To pursue such a course would be a blasphemy, an admission of defeat, and a negation of all our vows," Sato said, his protest made the more vehement by his own half-admitted doubts in the matter. In the first instance the idea of transferring the surviving mutated children to the Intensive Care Pediatric Unit, some five hundred kilometers from Main City, and isolated in the northern mountains of Ayoto, had been motivated by a faint hope that with care and treatment at least a small proportion of the monsters might be brought towards some kind of normality; but that hope had faded. Now it was apparent that the most the Intensive Care Unit could expect to do for the steadily growing number of patients was to feed and cleanse them, while they remained little more than mewling animals for the rest of their natural lives.

Mary Osawa sighed. "Perhaps you are right, Kenji. But there are already more than fifty of them. Yamaguchi and his people cannot cope with many more."

"I will talk with him, when I go there next week," Sato said. "There may be some way of easing the situation. In the meantime, I'd like you to take a look at this, particularly the section I have marked in red."

Mary Osawa scanned quickly through the draft of medical requirements prepared by the Explorations Division representatives. "A random sample of one thousand adults . . ." she quoted, looking up at Sato. "What does this mean? Do they know already?"

Sato shook his head. "I think not. According to the information I have been able to obtain about such investigations, this is merely a routine request. The actual numbers of subjects required for such testing is at the discretion of the Medical Officer in charge, and this Lieutenant Maseba is evidently a very thorough man. *We* shall have to be even more thorough."

"I don't understand." Mary Osawa frowned.

Sato leaned forward over his desk, speaking with soft urgency. "We can't possibly allow Maseba to examine a *truly* random sample, surely you can see that? It will be necessary to make a complete preliminary check on each person involved. No one with a history of Johannsen's disease, or who shows any positive trace of the presence of the virus, must be included."

"Preselection . . .?"

"By yourself and your team," Sato said. "It will be a big job, but not impossible for such an experienced group."

"And our research in the meantime?"

"I'm afraid that will have to wait," Sato said. "Believe me, I wouldn't involve you if there were anyone else qualified to do this job, but there just isn't. I could probably handle it myself, but that is impossible; there will be so many claims on my time and attention during this period. For one thing, I shall be expected to hold myself available at any time for liaison work with this Maseba."

Mary Osawa looked steadily into the strained face of this man for whom she had so much respect, both personally and professionally. Although what he asked of her was both dangerous and illegal, she was well aware that he asked not for himself, but for the planet of their birth.

"Very well, Kenji" she said. "I will do what is necessary. God grant that we are doing the right thing."

"Amen to that," Sato said, bowing his head.

This evening the garden was of little comfort to Kenji Sato. He felt weary in mind and body as he walked into the house; apprehensive of the web of intrigue in which he was already involved, and of the way in which that web must surely grow during the next few months.

As he removed his shoes, he heard a slight sound behind him, and turned, to see his wife Tana standing in the hallway.

"Kenji, my dear, we have visitors. Will you come and greet them now, or would you prefer to bathe and change first?"

Visitors . . . there was something about the way in which Tana pronounced the word, combined with the troubled expression on her usually placid face, which kindled a new apprehension in him.

"Visitors?"

"A girl, Mia Mizuno, of our own family, and the man who is to be her husband."

"Mizuno?" he repeated. It was an old name, with family associations that stretched back long before his own birth, to the family roots back on Earth. There were Mizunos here on Kepler, but none, so far as he knew, related to him. "I had better come and meet them now," he said.

The girl and her man were seated in the lounge with Yoko as he entered. Both were wearing the shapeless coveralls of Keplerian workers. The girl was a pretty little thing who might well have been Yoko's sister, but from the ungainly manner in which he rose to his feet from the *tatami* floor, the man was obviously a Westerner, despite his dark coloring.

The girl approached and bowed respectfully. "My apologies for this sudden intrusion, Sato-san. I am Mia Mizuno, of your family, from Haneda port, Tokyo, Earth. And this is my husband-to-be, Piet Huygens."

"Who is also from Earth?" Sato said, smiling up at the tall stranger, who stood awkwardly by. The smile was merely a formal one, a means of hiding the turbulence of his thoughts as he considered the possible implications of this visit. There had been no landing of an Earth-side ship on Kepler III since the Excelsior Corporation freighter *Wangituru* some three months previously, except that of the Space Corps ship *Venturer Twelve*. And yet these two were not dressed in Corps uniform, or in the kind of civilian clothes one would expect to find official passengers on such a ship wearing.

"From the North American continent, Lake Cities," Mia said. Bowing again, she held out in both hands an object elaborately wrapped in blue plastofoil. "Sato-san, I beg you to accept this worthless gift, and pray that you will listen with kindness to the story I have to tell of our reasons for being here."

"Where family is concerned, there can be no more sacred or true reason than the ties of blood," Sato said, bowing in return. "You are welcome to my humble house." He placed the gift on a small table, and spoke to his wife. "Our kinsfolk will take tea with us, Tana, my dear. Perhaps Yoko would assist you?"

As mother and daughter disappeared obediently from the room, Sato motioned to his guests to resume their sitting position, and squatted down himself opposite them. Now that the formalities were over he was anxious to know the full reasons behind the unheralded appearance of these two people from Earth.

"Huygens?" Commander Bruce glared up at Maseba.

"I'm afraid it looks that way," Maseba said, his dark face solemn. "No one has seen him aboard since last evening, and there's a record of his going planet-side at nineteen-thirty hours. Of course, there may be some very good reason . . ."

"Good reason? Damn and blast, man!" snapped Bruce. "There's no possible reason for a Corps officer to be absent from his post."

"An accident?" suggested Lindstrom.

"Then we would have been informed by the planetary authorities," Bruce said.

Maseba said, "I have to agree with you, Commander. I think we must treat this as a case of desertion and make the fair assumption that it is connected with the similar disappearance of Crewwoman Mizuno."

"Mizuno and Huygens?" Lindstrom said, looking at Maseba.

The Surgeon Lieutenant nodded. "Yes, and I'm afraid that I must be in some measure to blame for precipitating the crisis. You see, I ordered Huygens to carry out the Comp. Ab. on the girl."

"You mean the child is his?" Lindstrom said. "God! What a terrible thing for them both."

Bruce stared from one to the other of his two companions, an expression of incredulity on his rugged features. "Crossing ranks, illegal pregnancy, and now desertion, on *my* ship!" He jabbed a button on his desk. "Telecoms? Get me a vidphone link with the Main City Chief of Police."

"Commander, you agreed with Mr. Magnus . . ." began Lindstrom.

Bruce wheeled on her, his green eyes sparking with rage. "Against my better judgment, I agreed to withhold further action in the case of Mizuno, because of her race. Now that Huygens is involved the situation is changed. I want those two caught. And when they are, I'll throw the book at them. Ninety-nine percent of the Corps don't need encouragement to do their duty, but I'll see to it that those who do will have a salutary example in Mizuno and Huygens."

The girl seemed to sense his uneasiness. "Doctor Sato, we have no intention of becoming a permanent burden to you. But if we could at least stay for a few days . . ."

Sato's smile was a formal mask hiding his troubled thoughts. The story the girl had told him was appealing and intensely human, and he had no doubt of her sincerity. None but the hardest heart could refuse to have pity for two such star-crossed lovers in their attempt to escape from the pressures of a society that threatened to force them apart, and destroy the child of their love. Under normal circumstances he would have done what he could to help without the slightest hesitation.

"Of course, my child," he said gently. "That is the least I can do for a member of my family who has come so far. I was trying to think ahead. You see, as Minister of Health, I shall be intimately involved in the independence investigations, dealing with the very people who will be searching for you both. This makes me wonder if any help I may be able to offer you might not be more than counterbalanced by the jeopardy in which association with me must place you."

"That's not exactly true, Doctor Sato," Huygens said. "In the main you will be dealing with Explorations Division personnel, under the direct command of Magnus; whereas our desertion is, and will be treated as, a Corps matter. In that respect, the usual procedure is for the ship's commander to ask for the cooperation of the local police. I hardly think a man in your position would have much difficulty in dealing with them?"

Sato looked at Huygens, conscious of a rising dislike. Mia Mizuno's husband-to-be was a big man, who would stick out like a palm tree in scrubland among Keplerian society, despite any cosmetic adjustments. But even more important than outward appearances, there was an arrogant directness in Huygen's manner which branded him as alien. Half-ashamed of the racial prejudice that colored these private thoughts, Sato made a special effort to be courteous. "You are right, of course, Huygens-san. I am not without some little influence, and I shall naturally use it on behalf of yourself and Mia. Even so, it seems quite obvious that neither of you will be able to lead a normal social existence during the period of the investigation; and such confinement may well be a strain."

"But afterwards, we will at least be free," said Mia. "And Piet, with his Earth-training in medicine, will surely be a useful new citizen for Kepler III, even if I myself do not have a very valuable contribution to make."

In the face of the girl's becoming female modesty, Sato's smile was no longer formal. "My dear child, you would make a valuable contribution to any society by the very presence of your beauty and grace. You may both stay here, as long as you wish, under my protection."

"Oh, thank you, Sato-san . . ."

Sato waved aside her thanks, as he rose to his feet. "We shall not talk of this again. As far as our neighbors are concerned, Yoko will tell them that you are cousins on vacation from Minashu, and they will accept you as such."

"Thank you, Doctor Sato," said Huygens. "But we have no wish to be a burden to you. I had hoped that there might be some medical work I could do to repay your kindness."

"Later, of course," Sato said. "But for the time being I'm afraid it would be better if your undoubted professional abilities remained unrevealed. Now, if you will excuse me, I will go and change."

After a word with Yoko and Tana, who were preparing the evening meal, he retired to the comforting ritual of bathing. It was only when, having soaped and cleansed himself, he was relaxing in the delightfully hot, clean water of the bath, that a new and alarming possibility occurred to him. While he could not find it in himself to doubt the sincerity of Mia Mizuno, was it not possible that the girl had been duped, manipulated into just this situation, as part of some elaborate plot to plant a Corps spy in his household at this crucial time?

Bruce sat at his desk, his mouth a tight line as he studied the typescript of a speech he was to deliver at the civic banquet to be held in his honor in Central City that evening. The script had been prepared by the Explorations Division public relations experts under the personal supervision of Magnus, and it was, as might be expected from its origin, a superb piece of rhetoric stressing the interdependent roles of the colonies and United Earth in the glorious future of the human race. Basically, there was little that Bruce disagreed with in the speech, but it was alien to his nature to express himself in such a manner.

Picking up a felt-tipped pen, he began to go through the sheets, taking some pleasure in ruthlessly editing out some of the more fulsome phrases. He was disturbed in his task as the door opened and Lieutenant Lee Ching appeared.

Lee saluted smartly. "All correct, sir."

"Got your men?"

"Yes, sir."

"Arms?"

"Stunners, as ordered, sir."

"Good. Now you know the drill. First you call on Colonel Hitachi and tell him that we want the cooperation of his police in a search of the European sector of Central City, in the Kurile Street area."

"Hitachi knows we are coming, sir?"

"He was unavailable when I called," Bruce said. "But I spoke to his deputy, so they'll be expecting you. It seems obvious to me that, if Huygens is in hiding, he would be most likely to try to do so among his own kind, where he wouldn't be quite so conspicuous."

"And Mr. Magnus, sir?"

"Is away in New Honshu for the day. In any case, Corps discipline is my province, and I intend to make certain that it's enforced. Clear?"

"Yes, sir."

"Right—get moving."

Lee saluted and left.

Bruce returned his attention to the typescript. The first three of its neat pages were now scored by a number of uncompromising black slashes. He turned over to page four, the felt pen moving once more to its task as the banal phrases leapt up at him: "glorious tradition"—slash; "brotherhood of mankind"—slash. Magnus must have known quite well that he would never stand up in public and give voice to such hogwash. . . .

Bruce stopped, the pen poised, as a disquieting thought hit him. Of course Magnus would anticipate his objections to such tub-thumping oratory, and would expect him to edit the script accordingly; to edit out the fulsome rubbish, and be left eventually with . . . with just the speech Magnus really intended him to make.

Damn Magnus! He thrust the script to one side. The man's efficiency was becoming oppressive.

. . . But they are somewhere.
They have to be. By all the laws of probability,
We should have met them before. There,
Long before we reached the Rim, we should have
    found them.
Consider the odds. We cannot be
The only men. . . .

Kilroy: I. Kavanin

Ahead, where the massive grandeur of snow-capped northern Ayoto mountains rose abruptly from the valley floor, the buildings of the Intensive Care Pediatric Unit were still invisible behind the screening trees.

Seated beside the pilot as the copter scurried across the morning sky, Kenji Sato looked down on the deep green of the wooded valley, his drawn face somber with a familiar dread.

The site for the hospital had been carefully chosen. There were no roads, not even an isolated farmstead any nearer than sixty kilometers. All personnel and supplies were ferried in and out by this single copter which operated a shuttle service between the hospital and the small town of Ranaku, some eighty-five kilometers south. Even the inquisitive Mr. Magnus could surely find nothing to attract his interest in this virgin, wooded country, other than its scenic beauty, and Magnus was too fully occupied with more urgent matters. If isolation equated security, then the Intensive Care Unit was surely secure, and the dread which fell like a pall over Sato's thoughts had nothing to do with any doubts on that score.

More terrible than any remote possibility of prying by unwanted eyes were the memories of what he had seen here in the past, and would shortly see again; the pitiful, helpless creatures who depended entirely on the devoted care of Joni Yamaguchi and his staff; monstrous genetic sports whose very existence mocked the imagination of any God-made man. To most of the people of Kepler III, people who hid their true feelings with sayings like "catch a cold and find a monster," the Johannsen's-disease-mutated children were still mercifully only creatures of rumor; and even to those who had personal contact, through the accident of such a birth in their immediate family, that contact was a brief one, soon ended by the hurried removal of the child by discreet, white-jacketed strangers. There was no such release for Kenji Sato. As the copter arced in for its landing and the cluster of wooden buildings came into sight behind the trees, he reminded himself once again that one of the mewling, helpless animals being cared for in this sanctuary was his own grandchild.

The copter settled on the mossy grass about a hundred meters from the main building, its motors dying with a coughing whine. The pilot slid open the doors of the cabin, admitting a breeze laden with the scent of the trees of the forest and effervescent with the coolness of the mountain snows.

"You go ahead, doctor," he said. "And tell Billy Kanu to get the lead out and bring a truck over for this stuff. Like he expects I should dump it over there?" He nodded towards the pile of packaged supplies stacked at the back of the tiny cabin.

Sato smiled his assent, and stepped out onto the yielding grass. Here, with the great silence of a natural paradise broken only by the soughing of a breeze through the living green of the forest, the buildings, constructed from the wood of that same forest, merged with their surroundings, but man was still an intruder. Sato walked slowly up the gentle slope towards the main building, watching the verandah expectantly for the appearance of Yamaguchi, who must have heard the sound of the hovering copter. Yamaguchi was a brilliant young doctor, who had given up the prospect of a glittering career in Central City to take control of the Intensive Care Unit, but Sato was aware that even such dedication must falter eventually in the face of a hopeless task. If only he had been able to bring some ray of hope, some suggestion that the work of Mary Osawa and her virologists offered at least some possibility of checking the steadily growing incidence of monstrous births.

Sato stopped, frowning, as he reached the foot of

the verandah steps, sensing an unusual absence of familiar noises from within the building. Usually there was the sound of a typist, the murmur of voices, or the cry of a child, but today there was nothing but a dead silence. Morale might be bad at this time, but surely someone must have heard the approach of the copter?

Quickening his pace, he walked up the wooden steps towards the open main doorway. On the verandah, his foot encountered a yielding obstacle. He looked down, and saw a child's doll lying on the bare boards. Such toys were commonplace at the hospital, where every attempt was made to bring the monstrous children into contact with normal human life.

He bent down and picked up the doll. It was dressed in a miniature green silk kimono. The head had been crushed out of all human semblance, an act which must have entailed the exertion of brutal force, considering the durability of the plastic of which it was made. A deliberate act of destruction, the heavy grinding of a heel, perhaps. Sato held the doll looking down at its ruined face, conscious of a prickling feeling of apprehension which crawled its way over his scalp.

Inside, the chair by the reception desk and switchboard usually attended by Yamaguchi's secretary was vacant. The door of the medical director's office was to the left. Sato rapped briefly and walked in. The room was empty, but Sato noticed that the pilot light of the dictating machine was still glowing, as if Yamaguchi had stepped out in the middle of a memo, and carelessly omitted to switch the machine off. But Yamaguchi was not a careless man.

Sato turned abruptly and walked out of the room, conscious of the hollow sound of his own footsteps as he moved past the reception desk down the corridor which led to Ward A. The doors swung open at his approach and he strode into the ward, where the older of Yamaguchi's charges, the three-year-olds, were kept. The room was light and airy, with pastel-painted walls dotted with the kind of pictures one might expect to see in the nursery of any human child; cartoons of animals native to Kepler III or to faraway Earth, and happy, laughing children.

The children on the walls were the only ones to be seen in the ward. The bedclothes on the ten high-sided cots, five spaced on each side of the center aisle, were rumpled in disorder, but there was no sign of their occupants. Sato stood, held in a shock of incomprehension, his eyes surveying the deserted ward.

Hearing the sound of heavy footsteps behind him, he wheeled as the doors opened again to admit the copter pilot. The man's round face was questioning.

"Say, what's going on here, doctor? I got a load back there in the copter . . ." He ceased speaking and looked at Sato curiously.

Sato realized belatedly that he was still holding the mutilated doll in his left hand. He placed it down on a nearby cot. "You left last night for Ranaku?"

"Yes, sure. That's the routine," said the pilot.

"And there was no sign of anything unusual then?"

"No . . ."

"I'll take the other wards. You make a search of the living quarters," Sato ordered, moving towards the door, although he already had a feeling that the exercise was a pointless one. "I'll meet you back here in ten minutes."

In the other buildings the same enigma was repeated. There was no sign of disorder, everything appeared to be absolutely normal—save that there were no patients, or staff. Sato returned to the main building to find the copter pilot sitting on the steps of the verandah.

"Nothing, doctor, not a single human being in the whole place." The man shivered, as he looked up at Sato. "My girl, Asura, I went to her room, and there was nothing. For God's sake, what happened here?"

Sato could offer no explanation, even to himself. The

entire situation was quite beyond reason. There was no obvious reason for the evacuation of the hospital; if what had happened had indeed been an evacuation. In any case, where could the people have gone? Into the forest? Or up into the mountains? Moving, as they must, on foot, because the copter, their only transport, was not available. But even if the people of the staff had done such a thing—what of the fifty helpless patients, none of whom, as far as he knew, were capable of purposeful movement on their own account? The whole thing was inconceivable—and yet it had happened. Suddenly, the monstrous children had apparently been spirited away, as if they had never existed—and with them, thirty adult human beings, twenty of whom had been trained medical staff who could ill be spared. Unless . . .

Sato was conscious of a dreadful, cold rage growing in his mind. To President Kido, with his ambitions for the future of the planet, the mutated children had been a burden and a possible source of embarrassment. Kido had hinted more than once that he considered the policy of preservation a wasteful and dangerous one. What more likely than that, under fear of what the scrutiny of Magnus and the Explorations Division staff might reveal, Kido had steeled himself to take the ruthless, inhuman step of removing the monstrous children to some place where they would be exterminated en masse? It was an operation well within the capabilities of the forces directly under the command of the president, and it was almost surely in tune with his ruthless determination to maintain himself in power.

Under such circumstances, it was possible that Yamaguchi and his staff were unharmed, that Kido was merely intending to keep them out of sight in some safe place until the independence investigation was over. But the children—that monstrous but sacred trust . . .

"Take me back to Ranaku—at once!" Sato said to the copter pilot.

Tom Bruce stood on a balcony of the presidential palace holding a lukewarm glass of *sake* in his right hand and thinking longingly of what he would give for the taste of bourbon on the rocks. The humming chatter of the thronging crowds in the palace gardens below wafted up to him, making him thankful that he had at least managed to escape with the VIP attendees of the reception to the comparative quiet of the president's lounge.

"Ah, there you are, commander. Everything all right?"

Bruce turned, to find himself looking into the sallow moon-face of President Kido. "Very comfortable, thank you, Mr. President," he said, an automatic smile creasing his craggy features.

"Good! Good!" beamed the president. "I must tell you that your speeches so far have made a profound impression on our people. It is seldom that a man of action like yourself combines such powers of oratory with his other talents."

"You are too kind, Mr. President," Bruce said. That was the trouble; they were all too damned kind, and polite. Everybody on Kepler III smiled all the time, and each person he met vied with the other in the utterance of embarrassingly fulsome compliments. Despite the fact that Ichiwara, Magnus's assistant, had briefed him carefully on the Japanese habit of using speech to conceal rather than reveal one's true thoughts, Bruce found that the reality beggared the description. Social life on Kepler III was like constant total immersion in a barrel of molasses.

The president lowered his rotund body into a chair,

and motioned Bruce to take another close by him. Bruce obeyed. The prospect of yet another exchange of meaningless platitudes chafed as much as his over-tight full-dress uniform, but one just didn't walk out on a president.

"I have been meaning to ask you, commander," Kido said; "is my Colonel Hitachi giving you all the cooperation you need?"

"He was been most helpful," Bruce said truthfully. "But I'm afraid results so far haven't been encouraging. The fugitives seem to have disappeared into thin air."

"Ah, well, a minor matter," Kido said, waving one fat hand on which a ring with a diamond as big as an ice cube glittered. "After all, you are better off without such people. I would wish that some of my own malcontents might disappear so conveniently."

"Malcontents, here on Kepler?"

Kido's great belly shook, jellylike, as he chuckled. "My dear commander, you look shocked. Please forgive me for mentioning the subject."

"No . . . not at all. It is merely that everyone I have met here appears to be well contented and happy."

"Ah, everyone you have met, perhaps," said the president. "But I fear that, even in paradise, there are those who would find some cause for complaint, and Kepler III, despite the efforts of three generations of our people, is still not quite a paradise."

Bruce surveyed the bland features of his host thoughtfully. It would be interesting to know just where Shanon Kido stood in the private assessment of Charles Magnus, and what plans Magnus had for the president's future if, and when, independence was granted to the planet. As far as Bruce himself was concerned, the very fact that Kido was a politician was sufficient to make him uneasy and mistrustful in the man's presence.

"An interesting point of view, Mr. President," Bruce said. "Although it seems . . ."

He stopped talking as a thin man wearing a dark blue zipper-suit burst through the open doorway and hurried across to Kido.

"Mr. President, I have to talk with you—now!" The man's voice crackled with tension.

A shadow of irritation passed over Kido's Buddha-like features. "Doctor Sato, please. This is hardly the time . . ."

"Let me be the judge of that, Mr. President. I have just returned from Minaku, and . . ."

"Dr. Sato, you are discourteous in the extreme," Kido interrupted sharply. "I am entertaining an honored guest."

The man wheeled and saw Bruce for the first time.

"Commander Bruce, this is Doctor Sato, my Minister of Health," said Kido.

"Commander," Sato bowed slightly. "I must apologize for the intrusion."

"Dr. Sato," Bruce said, rising to his feet, noting the grayish pallor of the man's bony features, and the agitation flickering in his deep-set eyes.

"Mr. President, please . . ." Sato turned back to Kido. "I'm sure the commander will excuse us . . ."

"Gentlemen, I think it would be better if I left you to your business," Bruce said. "Obviously it is a matter of some urgency."

"No, no, Commander Bruce," said Kido, maneuvering his bulky body out of the chair in which he had been sitting. "Doctor Sato and I will retire to my study. Please make yourself comfortable."

Bruce watched curiously as the oddly assorted couple walked through the doorway into the lounge, wondering what kind of an emergency could have produced such an interruption.

"Doctor Sato, I find your suggestion that any such evacuation might have taken place under my direction slanderous, to say the least," President Kido said.

Kenji Sato, his first rage dissipated, sat on the edge of a chair, an increasing feeling of helplessness enveloping him as he searched the round, indignant features of the president.

Kido continued righteously: "I would remind you that the Intensive Care Unit was set up under your guidance, and run under your supervision. Therefore I suggest that whatever may have gone wrong there must be directly your own responsibility."

Sato bowed his head. "You're right, of course, Mr. President. The least I can do under the circumstances is to offer my resignation . . ."

"Resignation? Nonsense, man! What possible good could that do? Kepler III needs you, Doctor Sato. Now, let us consider this matter rationally, and see if we can arrive at some explanation. You say that there was no sign of violence at the hospital, that nothing had been disturbed?"

"Apart from the broken doll, and that could have been an accident," Sato said. "It would seem that the evacuation, if that is what it was, was carried out quite peaceably, with the cooperation of Yamaguchi and his staff."

"I take it that you discard outright the idea that Yamaguchi himself might have decided for some reason to abandon the hospital?"

"Don't you?" Sato said. "Sixty kilometers to the nearest town, through densely wooded country."

"And the alternative?"

"The arrival of a well-organized force, with the necessary transport, and documents capable of proving to Yamaguchi's satisfaction that it was his duty to co-operate."

"I have already assured you that no such operation has been mounted with my knowledge."

"It could hardly have been without," Sato said.

"I'm not entirely sure of that," Kido said, frowning thoughtfully. "There has been considerable to-and-fro-ing from *Venturer Twelve,* the Corps ship—especially since this business of the desertion of two of their crew members."

Sato nodded.

"Hitachi's police have been cooperating, of course. But there have also been a considerable number of flights by aircraft from the Corps ship in which our people have not been directly involved. It occurs to me that one of these search parties could have come upon the Intensive Care Unit by accident, and gone down to investigate."

"So far north?"

Kido shrugged massively. "The remoteness of the region might well be the very factor which caused them to search there."

"You realize what you're suggesting," Sato said. "If that is what happened then why haven't the investigating team informed us?"

"Then let us pray that I am wrong," said the president. "If such an operation has been carried out, we are unlikely to hear anything of it from Magnus until he has investigated the matter fully and is completely sure of his ground."

"And our hopes of gaining independence smashed beyond possibility of retrieval," Sato said. "This Com-mander Bruce with whom you were talking. He would surely know?"

"The Explorations Division officer is an extremely devious man," Kido said. "I doubt very much whether he would have taken the brave commander into his con-fidence at this stage."

"Then we must do as I suggested before, and approach Magnus without further delay, giving him the full story."

"And throw ourselves on his mercy?" Kido said. "No, Doctor Sato, that would be foolhardy until we are sure that this is the correct explanation of the incident."

"Then what should we do?"

"You must continue with your work as before, and leave the matter to me, Sato. In the meantime, I shall speak with Colonel Hitachi and have him send a squad of investigators to the Intensive Care Unit. There may be some traces, some clues about the nature of the evacuation which you missed during your visit."

COM QXYPRL to BIOCOM H.Q. 15/67/789

SAMPLE SPECIMENS COLLECTED AS PER INSTRUCTIONS. OPERATION SUCCESSFUL WITH MINIMUM DISTURBANCE OF ENVIRONMENT. BIPEDAL UNITS IN IMMEDIATE AREA ELIMINATED.

EXAMINATION OF SPECIMENS WITH REFERENCE TO SPECIFICATIONS PROJECT BIOCOM VX2541D NOW PROCEEDING. REPORT SCHEDULED FIFTEEN CYCLES FROM NOW.

When Mia came in, Piet was squatting on the edge of the *futon* bedding. He was wearing the thin white sleeping suit which Tana Sato had bought for him at the local market, and which, being made to average Kepler measurements, was far too small. He was holding a bottle in one hand and a glass in the other, and when she came close to him and kissed his ear she could smell the reek of alcohol.

"Piet . . ." He made no response, continuing to stare in front of him.

"Piet, what's the matter? What are you drinking?"

He held up the bottle, and looked at her with glazed eyes. "Vodka. Kepler-type vodka, but still average plus." His voice was slurred and thick.

She squatted beside him. "Once, you hardly drank at all."

"Once . . ."

"Piet, love—you're not drunk, are you?"

"No, not drunk—just bored and bloody useless," he said morosely.

"But where did you get the vodka?"

"Nearest thing they had to schnapps . . . down at the Magnolia bar, at the crossroads." He jerked a thumb.

"You went out?"

"Sure I went out," he said, with a touch of defiance. "You were busy talking and giggling with Yoko and Mrs. Sato. What else was there to do?"

"But we agreed . . ."

"Ah, where's the harm in it? Ten days stuck here in this damned doll's house with nothing to do but sit and think. It's worse than being in jail."

"But you know it's only temporary. When *Vee Twelve* has gone, Doctor Sato has promised to find work for you. We shall be Keplerians, free to do as we please, to come and go . . ."

He looked at her, the corners of his mouth downturned. "Citizens of the brave new world? I wonder . . ."

"Why, whatever do you mean?"

"I mean, if I keep on looking like this, with the crosscut eyes and the black hair, will I be looked on eventually as an insider?"

"I don't understand."

"No, I don't think you do," he said. "But whether you know it or not, right now I'm an outsider; the one

European in a household of Asiatics, and I can feel the prejudice. I can feel them watching me, and pitying me, when I pick up my rice bowl with the wrong hand, or when I fumble clumsily with my *hashi*, saying to themselves, 'Poor man, he does not know our ways . . .' "

"No, Piet, you're imagining it."

"The hell I am! When I came into the room this evening, you and Yoko were playing a game with wooden blocks, and you both looked up at me as though—just for a fraction of a second—as though you didn't know me . . . as though you had no need for me. Sometimes I think that, now you have the baby in your womb, maybe you don't; that my part is over, and now I'm nothing but a burden to you." He finished his drink at a gulp and slammed down the glass, staring deliberately away from her. Then, realizing that she had made no sound, he looked at her again.

She was regarding him with an apparently placid face, but tears streamed down her cheeks. The ice of his self-pity could do nothing but melt before her mute appeal. He took her in his arms, and she came to him, nestling against his chest.

"It's me, isn't it?" he said, talking to the dark top of her head. "I'm a mess, hadn't you realized that—a bloody mess! Call it lack of inner resource, latent instability, what you like, but I'm gradually going out of my mind here in this idleness. Back there on the ship, I was at least useful, I had some function, and there was a place for me in the scheme of things. Here . . ."

She moved away slightly, looking up at him, the tears drying on her cheeks. "You've changed your mind? You want to go back?"

"No! That's out of the question. There can be no going back now. Now I don't even belong there, and you . . ."

"Then what, Piet, love? I will do anything, anything at all."

He ran his fingers down her arm, feeling the warmth of her flesh, ashamed of the frustration that had made him cause her pain. "I know you would, my darling. But I think that at this stage there is nothing you can do. As you have said so many times, we must wait, and we must be patient. Doctor Sato will find me a position when the time is ripe, and I shall work, and all these misgivings will be forgotten."

"There would be something for you to do here, if you wished," she said.

He frowned. "What do you mean?"

"Yoko," she said. "There is a great fear in her heart about the birth of her child. As a doctor, you could talk to her, reassure her."

"All women must have certain fears during their first pregnancy. And I doubt that I can give her any better advice than that she must have had from her father."

"But this is not her first," Mia said. "There was another, nearly eighteen months ago . . ."

"Stillborn?"

"No—the child lived, but there was something, something wrong. Just what, she will not say, but it is away in some special hospital, under constant care."

"You're sure she has told you no details?"

"No—only that it was . . . different."

"Different . . ." he repeated, his mind suddenly alert, the alcohol-induced dullness sloughed away, as he began to think like a doctor again. When the word *different* was used to describe a child born on a planet like Kepler III, there was one obvious interpretation that sprang immediately to mind: *mutation,* the genetic effects of radiation from an alien sun. And yet the colony on Kepler had existed for a hundred years, with no reports of such genetic effects; the second and third generation colonists he had met were apparently normal in every respect. *Those he had met . . .*

"Piet, love, what are you thinking?" she asked.

He smiled a reassurance he did not feel. "Nothing, my darling—only, as you say, that there may be work for me here, after all."

COM QXYPRL TO BIOCOM H.Q. 29/67/789

REFERENCE EXAMINATION OF SAMPLE SPECIMENS RE PROJECT BIOCOM VX2541D. 15% PRODUCT VIABLE, BUT DEFINITELY SUBSTANDARD TO SPECIFICATIONS.

RESULTS INDICATE PROJECT VX2541D FAILURE, BUT VALUABLE DATA OBTAINED—SEE APPENDED SCHEDULE OF SUGGESTED EPISOME MODIFICATION.

REQUEST INSTRUCTIONS RE ENVIRONMENT AND FAUNA—SUGGEST DECONTAMINATION.

Tom Bruce was seated at the head of the table next to the Explorations Division officer. He found himself almost grateful that Magnus's carefully planned schedule included these working lunches during which the people in charge of the various aspects of the independence investigation were able to exchange ideas in an informal manner. Additionally, as his own daily program included at least one appearance as guest of honor at a Keplerian banquet, he was pleased to get back to the predictable plainness of Corps ship food. On one occasion the CPO chef, inspired by a visit to Central City, turned out an imitation Japanese meal, complete with mountains of boiled rice and raw fish. A brief interview with Bruce ensured that this flight of fancy was not repeated, and after that the content of the meals settled down to comfortable normalcy. Ichiwara had told Bruce that Japanese stomachs had, over many centuries, adapted themselves to a diet of *gohan,* with intestines a foot longer than the European normal, and an enquiry to George Maseba had confirmed this fact, adding the bonus suggestion that this was not so much a matter of special development as a clear example of natural selection, because people without the extra intestinal length tended to die off under the continued strain of such a diet. Bruce, convinced that his own stomach was irrevocably European, was attacking a sirloin steak with some pleasure.

"You mentioned Sato?" said George Maseba, who was sitting next to him on the other side. "A very strange little man. Most cooperative, and painfully polite, like the rest of his countrymen, but so terribly harassed . . . no, it's even more than that, he looks like a man who is haunted by some dreadful fear."

"You say he actually burst in on President Kido in the middle of a reception?" Magnus asked Bruce.

"Not quite that, there were only myself and Kido on the balcony. But I got the feeling that it wouldn't have made any difference if Kido had been in conference with God Almighty—Sato would have insisted on having his say."

Magnus eyed his underdone fillet reflectively. "Rather uncharacteristic for a Keplerian, wouldn't you say, Joseph?"

"One can only assume that Doctor Sato was under very considerable strain at the time," Ichiwara agreed. "Even so, such behavior would undoubtedly be frowned on as a serious breach of protocol. To display such unseemly urgency in the presence of a person of high rank . . ."

"Tell me more about this Doctor Sato," Magnus said, addressing his question to Maseba, and saving those within earshot from listening to one of the eager Ichiwara's extended lectures on Japanese manners and customs.

"Well, let me put it to you this way," Maseba said. "If Sato were an officer aboard any ship of mine, I would immediately suspend him from active duty, and insist that he undergo psychotherapy."

"You're suggesting that he is a psychotic?"

"Well, now, I wouldn't commit myself to that extent," Maseba said. "But I would say that he has been under some constant strain for such a long period that his judgment may already be impaired, and that if the stress situation continues, he is likely to break down completely."

"Interesting . . ." murmured Magnus, thoughtfully. "We must give further consideration to the condition of Doctor Sato."

"While you're about it, you would do well to focus your attention on President Kido," Bruce said. "I have a feeling that he is an extremely devious and ruthless gentleman."

"A *feeling,* commander?" said Magnus.

"Let me put it this way," Bruce said. "If I were in charge of this independence investigation, I would consider it obligatory to make a very thorough study of the motives and actions of Kido."

"With what in view, commander?"

"Well—assuming that you are going to grant independence to Kepler III, you will be investing considerable extra power in the hands of Kido as its president-in-office by doing so. It seems to me, from the point of view of the future of the planet, that could be a serious mistake."

"President Kido is the democratically elected leader of the Keplerian people," Magnus said. "It would also be a mistake to interfere in the internal affairs of the planetary government on the basis of a sheer hunch, Commander. However, I shall bear your opinion in mind."

Bruce turned his attention to his plate, conscious of the flush of anger that suffused his cheeks. Damn Magnus! There were times when the man's patronizing manner was quite intolerable.

Kenji Sato woke in the darkness and waited for the meshing of the mental gears, the runaway acceleration of his mind as it began the usual fruitless playback of insoluble problems, a cycle which he was able to break only by drugging himself, or by abandoning the idea of sleep altogether and leaving his bed. He glanced at the luminous dial of his watch. Two A.M. He usually awoke around four. And this awakening was somehow different; by now his mind should have been racing through the endless labyrinth of unsolved problems like a maddened rat in a circular maze, but it wasn't; instead, there was an alertness. It occurred to him that for once the stimulus which had awakened him had been external rather than internal.

Careful not to disturb the still-sleeping Tana, he raised himself on one elbow, listening. The faint *chirr* of night insects, and above that another sound which stimulated recall of the one which had awakened him —the slight, familiar creak of the garden gate. Now he could hear someone, or some *thing,* making its way up the path towards the front door with slithering, unsteady footsteps.

Slipping carefully out from under the *futon* quilt, Sato paused only to pick up a pencil torch and a small needle gun, then hurried quietly out of the room towards the front of the house. Burglary was a rare, almost unheard of crime on Kepler, but these were strange times, and his own situation was an unusual one. Even now he could not be sure that Kido had been telling the truth about the disappearance of the inhabitants of the Intensive Care Unit; and whatever that truth might be, it was clear that there were unusual and desperate forces at work here on Kepler at this time.

Reaching the polished wooden floor of the hallway, he paused a few feet away from the front door, which was, in the customary manner, closed but not locked. Even had it been locked, a light structure of bamboo and lath, it would have offered little resistance to a determined intruder. In Keplerian society, the barriers of respect and etiquette were far stronger than any physical obstruction when it came to preserving personal privacy.

The footsteps were closer now, and he could hear the sound of heavy, grunting breathing. A moment later, a clumsy fumbling with the handle of the door, and it was thrust open abruptly. Sato stood for a moment, staring at the figure that loomed hugely in the rectangle of night sky revealed by the open doorway, then switched on his pencil torch.

"What the hell?" Piet Huygens blinked owlishly in the sudden glare, one hand clutching for support against the door lintel, the other grasping a bottle. Standing some six feet away, Sato was aware of the disgusting reek of second-hand alcohol. Lowering the torch, he moved quietly to the wall switch.

"Oh, it's you," said Huygens, as the light came on. "Did I wake you up? Sorry." With the exaggerated care of a drunk, he closed the front door. "Didn't mean to disturb anybody."

Sato made no attempt to hide his disapproval. One had responsibilities towards guests and family—but guests and family also had responsibility.

"Aw, now look here, Doc." Huygens began to move forward across the polished floor of the hallway, gingerly, like a man walking on thin ice.

"You will remove your shoes, please," Sato said quietly.

"My? Oh, yes—my shoes!" giggled Huygens. "Mustn't spoil the shine, must we?" Bending down, he went through an elaborate and unsteady pantomime, during which he twice overturned the bottle and twice placed it upright. Eventually barefoot, he picked it up again and stood, swaying slightly, regarding Sato through bleary, red-rimmed eyes.

"Well furcrysay, Doc, what you looking at me like that for? I didn't murder anybody, or anything—I'm just a bit stoned, that's all."

"The origin of your condition would be quite obvious, even to an untrained eye," Sato said stiffly. He came to a decision. "If you will join me in the lounge, there are certain matters we should discuss."

"This time of the morning?"

"As you have seen fit to wake me, yes, I think this time would be as good as any," Sato said.

In the lounge, Piet Huygens lowered himself clumsily to the *tatami*. The encounter had obviously sobered him slightly and he was sufficiently in control of his faculties to stare at Sato with some resentment.

"First I would like you to tell me where you have been," Sato said, squatting opposite Piet.

"The Magnolia bar, down at the crossroads."

"Until now?"

"I have friends down there," Piet said resentfully.

"Baba? Yes, I know of her. And from what I hear she is not a good woman."

"A good woman—hell, Doc, who spends till two o'clock in the morning with a *good* woman?"

"And your wife—Mia?"

"Ah, now look here . . ."

"All right—that is none of my business," Sato said. "But I must remind you that we decided when you arrived that it would be best for you to stay here in the house as much as possible, and not draw attention to yourself."

"So who's drawing attention? A few quiet drinks . . ."

"Possibly—but surely you must realize that the police keep such places under constant surveillance?"

"So you fix it, huh, Uncle Sato? You're the big man around here, aren't you? I mean, like Minister of Health, you've got a lot of pull, even if you are a pretty lousy medic, and you are trying to put one over on the independence investigator."

Sato felt a surge of anger at the jeering tone, and a flush of fear. "What do you mean?"

"Aw, come off it, Sato," Piet said, fumbling with a crumpled pack of cigarettes. "A fifth-rate virus infection like Johannsen's disease, and you can't lick it. I'm not surprised you're trying to keep it quiet, instead of asking for Magnus's help and revealing your incompetence."

"You know?"

Huygens lit a bent cigarette and exhaled a cloud of blue smoke. "Sure I know. You think I'm stupid, or something? 'Catch a cold and find a monster'—I heard that down at the Magnolia a few times, and I must admit that I didn't think of it as anything more than one of your cute Keplerian sayings until Mia mentioned about Yoko, and her first baby. Then I decided it was time I had a little chat with your darling daughter."

"You talked to Yoko—what about?"

"Her pregancy, of course. It was quite clear from what Mia had told me that the poor girl was in need of some kind of reassurance."

"Reassurance? What have you been telling her?" demanded Sato.

"Just that her fears are quite groundless, and that there's no possible reason why she shouldn't bear a normal child now that the disease is out of her system."

"You had no business to interfere."

"On the contrary—I felt that I had a duty to do so," Huygens said. "As her father and physician it seems to me that you've been doing a pretty poor job of reassuring her."

"You may be right, but you should have talked with me first," Sato said.

"With you? When do I ever see you, for God's sake?" Huygens said. He appeared comparatively sober now, as he leaned forward. "Look here, Sato, how much longer do you think I can stand being cooped up doing absolutely nothing? I have professional training and ability, all of it going to waste. Can't you see I want to help?"

"I explained before, that is impossible at this stage. When *Venturer Twelve* has left Kepler, and the independence investigation is over . . ."

"No, *now!*" Huygens said forcefully. "You've got yourself tied in knots over this Johannsen's business. What's the matter—don't you trust me?"

The bluntness of the challenge made Sato once more aware and ashamed of his own prejudice. There was no real reason to suppose that Huygens was anything other than what he appeared to be, and yet. . . . He hesitated.

"Look, for a start, you could at least tell me the real reason you haven't reported the incidence of Johannsen's disease to Magnus."

"Because the president has expressly forbidden me to do so—and for a very good reason," Sato said. "Explorations Division would be delighted to receive such a ready-made excuse to deny independence and deliver us back into the hands of the Excelsior Corporation."

Huygens squinted at his host through a cloud of tobacco smoke. "You really think that Explorations Division would do that?"

"It seems likely," Sato said. "After all, both organizations are Earth-based, with common links and interests."

Huygens shook his head, grinning. "Man, that just shows how little you know about what really goes on back home. You're looking at the whole thing from the wrong end—the Kepler end—of the telescope. If the corporations had their way, there wouldn't even *be* an Explorations Division. Then they could really start to milk the colonial planets in earnest. Magnus isn't here to rob you of your precious independence—he's just as anxious as you are that Kepler should qualify. United Earth needs strong, independent colonies who will stand by her, not rebellious subject-planets starved of development ready to stab her in the back at the first opportunity."

Sato recognized that his point of view was parochial, but it was one which he shared with the majority of Keplerians. Despite the outward show of welcome for Magnus and *Venturer Twelve,* it was natural that after a century of thralldom to the Excelsior Corporation's cold commercialism there should be some distrust in Earth politics. "There may be some truth in what you say," he admitted, "but the decision not to be perfectly frank with Magnus was made at presidential level, and I have no authority to alter it."

"Pity," said Huygens. "Then it looks as though you're going to have to play this thing the hard way, even though there must be enough attenuated virus in *Vee Twelve's* stock to immunize the entire population of Kepler ten times over. Just how much Johannsen's do you have, anyway?"

"The incidence is comparatively small. There were twelve cases notified last month," lied Sato. He was well aware that the true figure had been nearer a hundred, and that in the first ten days of the present month, that number had already been passed, but he did not want to panic Huygens and send him howling back to *Venturer Twelve* with the story of a growing epidemic.

"Notified cases—but there must be others that you don't know about," Huygens said. "After all, apart from its effect on pregnant women, Johannsen's isn't a particularly incapacitating disease. It has been known for people to continue working right through an attack without realizing that they are suffering from anything more serious than a touch of common cold."

"That is possible," agreed Sato. He found that his innate dislike of Huygens was gradually being tempered by respect for the man's professional approach. Perhaps the solution to many of his problems had been lying here, in his own home, all the time.

"It would seem to me that the most important aspect as far as Kepler is concerned is the possible genetic effects of Johannsen's," Huygens said. "A colonial planet needs all the strong, healthy children it can produce, if it is to develop. If incidence is as low as you say, then there should be no difficulty in concealing the cases during the independence investigations, but that's only a part of the story. We've got to tackle the situation from the long-term point of view."

Huygen's use of the collective 'we' might be interpreted to mean that he was already identifying himself with the inhabitants of Kepler rather than the Space Corps, or United Earth, but Sato remained cautious. "My colleague, Mary Osawa, is working on the development of a serum at the present time."

"A serum?" Huygens regarded his host with some surprise. "We abandoned serum treatment of this kind of virus infection nearly a century ago back on Earth. I'm not absolutely sure of the figures, but I'd like to bet that any immunity provided by serums in a disease like Johannsen's wouldn't last more than a month or so, at most. The only really effective method is to develop an attenuated virus strain, and use that to enable the body to set up its own resistance system."

We're hick witch doctors to this bright young man with all Earth's training and confidence behind him, thought Sato. He has been at the center of medical research, where all the latest methods are at his fingertips. Whereas we, isolated here on our little ball of mud, light years from that center, can only grope towards solutions, using out-of-date methods.

"Sato, you've got to let me help you with this thing," persisted Huygens. "I did some research work on virology back in Lake Cities. Give me a laboratory and some competent technicians, and let me start work on the development of an attenuated strain right away. That's the only possible way in which this thing can be conquered."

Sato nodded wearily. "You may very well be right," he admitted. "But for the time being we must remember that you are still a fugitive. You must give me time to discuss this with my colleagues, and decide the best way in which matters can be arranged."

BIOCOM H.Q. TO COM QXYPRL   30/67/789

PROCEED WITH DECONTAMINATION IN ACCOR-
DANCE WITH STANDING ORDER NO. 5874X.
AFTERWARDS, RETURN TO BASE FOR FURTHER
INSTRUCTIONS.

Commander Bruce got out of his ground car at the main entrance of the Medical Inspection Center, a huge, temporary building which had been erected in Jokarta Park about five kilometers from the field where *Venturer Twelve* was berthed. Left with a mercifully free day from his seemingly endless round of public relations appearances, he had decided to take a look at how the medical part of the investigation was proceeding.

Leela De Witt looked up from her desk as he entered. "Hallo there, Commander," she said smiling, as she ran a hand through her short-cut, tousled dark hair. "No civic lunch today?"

Bruce grimaced. "Don't mention it. Another week of this and you're going to have to fit me up with a new stomach."

"Make it three weeks, and we may be able to squeeze you in," said Leela De Witt. "Right now we've got all the work we can handle with these examinations. You know what a stickler George Maseba is for detail, and with fifty subjects a day to get through we're on quite a treadmill here. If Huygens had been with us it would have been slightly easier, but as things are there's just no margin to relax."

"Huygens," Bruce repeated the name dourly. "Blasted young fool! Sacrificing everything, his career, his future, for what? Whatever got into him?"

"Whatever it was, it must have been planted deep down in his mind a long time ago," said De Witt. "Otherwise it would have shown up in his psyche processing. Strange how such instabilities can lie dormant until some particular set of circumstances trigger them off . . . his longing for security, and his basic discontent with his position in the Corps—those we knew about and could have handled, but for that one frayed link . . ."

"Discontent with the Corps?" Bruce's green eyes glinted. "He was a commissioned officer."

"A *medical* officer," Leela De Witt corrected him. "We're pretty short on medics, Commander. Which means that every now and again we have to compromise. Mostly it works out all right, but this time it didn't. Mind you, for a man like Piet Huygens, it won't anywhere, poor devil. He's the kind who gets dissatisfied, thinks the world owes him anything he chooses to want, and ends up by boozing himself insensible and sleeping with the first available woman. Then he comes back, weeping tears of remorse, because the world's bitched him again."

"He'll get remorse if I lay my hands on him," Bruce said grimly. "But at the rate the local police are working, there doesn't seem much fear of that."

"That's funny—we've found them most helpful and efficient," Leela De Witt said. "Each morning and afternoon a busload of subjects accompanied by an escort of police turns up for examination, no arguments, all tallying with the list received the previous day."

Bruce shrugged. "Maybe they're just better at organizing that kind of thing than actually searching for fugitives." He glanced at his watch. "Anyway, I take it that you're through with the morning batch? What time is the next one due?"

Leela De Witt rose to her feet. "We've got a couple of hours. I expect you'd like to have a word with George. Come with me and I'll take you to his den."

Surgeon Lieutenant George Maseba was less sanguine than his assistant about the progress of the mass examination. Bruce recognized the signs. Like himself, Maseba was a perfectionist, never content to accept the second rate in any form. As they drank coffee and ate sandwiches brought by the efficient Caiola, Maseba explained the problems of the present operation.

"What it amounts to is this—a routine physical examination, blood analysis, general radiography plates and a very brief psyche assessment—all done with reference to the record card supplied to us by the Keplerian Ministry of Health. In the really important business of genetic analysis there just isn't time to take more than a random sample, and hope that any significant irregularity will be revealed. But, you see, what this amounts to is making a random sample of a random sample—so that what we are getting is really too small a proportion of the total to be of any real significance."

"A detailed gene analysis of five percent of the sample must have some validity," Leela De Witt pointed out. "Statistically speaking, any significant mutation should show up in such a sample."

"Statistically speaking . . ." George Maseba rolled the whites of his eyes heavenwards in disgust.

"So what's the alternative?" De Witt persisted, with a hint of gentle chiding. "There just isn't time to take each and every one of the sample subjects apart one by one—and even if we did, going by your standards, we still wouldn't be happy, because even then we would be working on a statistical assumption."

"I don't follow you," queried Bruce.

"What I mean is that our one thousand examinees are still only point one percent of the total population," said Leela De Witt. "To be absolutely sure, in terms of the standards George seems to set himself, we would have to examine *every* human being on the planet."

"That's the devil of it," Maseba said. "What we're doing at the moment is a tremendous, wearing task—a routine, boring one which demands utter concentration, in case some significant detail should be missed. And yet at the same time I get this feeling that there must be a better way."

"Which you can't think of?" Bruce supplied.

Maseba reached over and poured the coffee. "Right. We're doing our best, but all the time there's this maddening conviction that our best just isn't good enough."

Bruce nodded his sympathy. He had a tremendous respect for Maseba's ability, and he could appreciate the man's dilemma.

"All right, so it's a treadmill," said Leela De Witt in her usual cheerful manner. "But we're not the only ones with troubles, and at least ours will be over when the investigation is completed."

"What do you mean?" asked Bruce.

"Well, look at the situation of the medics here on Kepler," De Witt said. "They must be worked to death. There are only two hundred and twelve practising general practitioners on Kepler—which means something like five thousand patients per doctor. Even though they're dealing with a basically healthy, sturdy people, they can't possible have an easy time of it. Certainly there must be little time for frills, and God knows what would happen here if there were some kind of epidemic."

It was at this point that George Maseba galvanized into action, startling his two companions. Leaping from his chair, he hurried across to his desk and began rummaging among the files there. A couple of minutes later, he punched a button on the intercom. "Caiola? No? Well get him—*now!* And tell him I want the record cards right away in my office. Why, sure, the ones supplied to us by the Kepler Ministry of Health— what others would I mean? No—not just those we've already examined—the lot!" He switched off and turned his attention back to De Witt and Bruce.

"What happened?" asked Bruce.

"I just had my eyes opened, that's all," Maseba said. "Thanks to a piece of morale-building chat from our lady-psyche here."

"What do you mean?" asked Bruce.

"Simply that these so-efficient Keplerians have been pulling the wool over our eyes all along," Maseba said, grimly. "I may be wrong—I hope I am, but I've got a feeling I'm not." He punched the intercom button again. "Caiola—get the lead out! Where are those damned record cards?"

"Oh, come on, Magnus," said Bruce. "It's quite obvious that they're trying to hide something. What other explanation could there be? With the number of doctors they have, it's not possible that every inhabitant of Kepler III could have been subjected to a routine medical examination during the last month—such an operation would take six months, at least. And yet when we examined the record cards of the sample, everyone had undergone just that. Surely that makes it quite obvious that these people were carefully selected beforehand?"

"There may be something in what you say, commander," Magnus said calmly. "But we must not jump to conclusions."

Maseba shook his head. "I wouldn't have had the slightest objection if a small proportion had undergone such an examination—that would be normal procedure; but to discover that *all* of them had done so goes way beyond the possibilities of coincidence. It seems to me that they were carefully selected for some reason, and the most obvious explanation I can think of is that they are free of some factor which is present in a large proportion of the population, and which the Keplerian government is determined to hide from us."

"Some factor?" repeated Magnus.

Maseba shrugged. "Mutation, disease, mental instability—I can only guess at the moment. If I can get my hands on a *truly* random sample, then perhaps I shall be able to tell you more."

"What do you intend to do about your present examination schedule?"

"I think it may be best for the present to continue with the operation, but it seems obvious to me that any results we may obtain must be quite useless," Maseba said.

Magnus nodded. "Good! We don't wish to spread undue alarm until we have all the facts. Obviously the Keplerians are in a state of anxiety at the present time, and it would be foolish to move percipitately."

"But you're going to do something, surely?" demanded Bruce. He was irritated by the Explorations Division officer's smooth, diplomatic manner.

Magnus raised one eyebrow. "You have some suggestion, perhaps, Commander?"

"You're damned right I have! Let me send out a couple of squads and have them bring in the first fifty civilians they can grab. Then ship them over to the examination center and let Maseba and his boys run the rule over them."

"Commander! Such tactics are quite unthinkable— the kidnapping of fifty innocent civilians, citizens of a friendly colony . . ."

"If that's the only way Maseba is likely to get a *really* random sample, why not?" Bruce said.

"And suppose this so-far unidentified factor he is looking for failed to make an appearance in any of these fifty Keplerians—what then, commander? At the very least we would have sacrificed any good will that might have existed between ourselves and the Keplerian government—and at the worst, we would probably have massive riots on our hands led by the relatives of those people we had kidnapped."

Maseba shook his head. "He's right, you know, Tom. There's absolutely no guarantee that this X factor, whatever it may be, will turn up in a sample of fifty, or even a hundred. Point one percent is the absolute minimum working sample in an investigation of this kind . . . and you can't kidnap a thousand people. Even if you could, we wouldn't be able to examine them in under a month—and that's quite impractical."

"All right, so what *do* we do?" demanded Bruce.

"You, Commander Bruce, will continue with your public relations schedule, and Surgeon Lieutenant Maseba will go on with his examination of the sample provided by the Keplerian Ministry of Health," said Magnus. "In the meantime, I shall pay a visit to President Kido and discuss the situation with him. I'm sure we shall be able to come to some sensible conclusion. And now, gentlemen, if you will excuse me." Magnus bent his head, pointedly transferring his attention to the files on the desk in front of him.

Piet stirred, and found that he was alone. From somewhere in the night he heard the slam of a door, and the whirr of a ground car engine going away. There was a shadow by the window. Switching on the bed-side lamp, he said: "Mia? What is it?"

Mia turned and walked towards him with the careful straddle of a heavily pregnant woman. She lowered her-self down beside him slowly. "Yoko; I think it's her time. That was Doctor Sato taking her off to the hos-pital."

Piet shook his head. "We could have delivered that baby, here in her own home. But no—Sato has to be stubborn about it, and ship her off to some aseptic mausoleum of a hospital."

"He wants her to have the best possible care."

"Maybe, but in her state of mind it would have been better to have let her remain in familiar surroundings, with her mother nearby. It's very unlikely that the birth will be anything other than a completely normal one, but the traumatic effects on Yoko herself could be distrastrous."

"His own daughter, Piet. . . . He must have con-sidered the situation carefully before making his de-cision."

Piet scowled. "I just hope so. Sometimes I wonder about your Uncle Sato. Maybe it's this old cultural bar-rier thing, but half the time I just can't follow his reasoning at all."

"He has tremendous responsibilities," Mia said de-fensively.

"Then why doesn't he let me help ease the burden?"

Mia sighed. "Strange, isn't it? We're so very different, despite everything. To me, it seems quite logical that Doctor Sato should act the way he does—and yet I can't explain my reasons to you, the person I love most of all in the whole universe."

Feeling a sudden rush of tenderness, he reached out and took her tiny hand in his own. "Just remember that, and I'll ask for no more explanations," he said.

She smiled down at him. "I don't feel a bit sleepy. I think I'll go and make some tea. Like some?"

"Please." He released her, and she rose from the *futon* again, walking towards the window.

She stayed there for a moment looking out.

"What is it?" he asked.

"The moonlight looked suddenly bright. Those two moons . . . I think I'll never get used to them. Oh, Piet, come here!"

He was by her side at once, looking out into the hazy moonlight. From where they stood they could see the road to Tamah through the shrubs and trees of the garden. The evenly spaced street lamps seemed somehow dimmer . . .

Piet looked into the sky as the moonlight appeared to brighten. As he watched, a point of light detached itself from the smaller of the two satellites, grew, lengthened, became thin and suddenly extended itself downwards like a needle of impossibly straight lightning.

"Down!" Piet shouted, as he threw himself to the floor, turned, and caught Mia as she came down after him, cushioning her body with his own. The room was lit by a huge orange glow, and it seemed as though the breath from a gigantic furnace suddenly puffed at the house, shattering the laminated windows, crackling as it seared through the bushes and small trees outside. For a few seconds the rushing, hellish wind tore past the house; then it faded, but the glow outside remained.

Piet got to his feet. "Stay there a minute!" he ordered Mia, as he looked out of the window again.

The Tamah crossroads were no longer there. Instead, in a rough circle a hundred meters across, there was a bubbling cauldron of fire, evil and orange-yellow, which crackled, hissed and swirled. The houses of the village center, the Magnolia bar, had totally disappeared.

There came an excited knocking on their door, and the hysteria-laden voice of Tana Sato. "Mia—Piet—are you all right?"

Piet opened the door. "You stay with Mia, Mrs. Sato. I'm going to see what is going on down there! I may be able to help."

Dressing hurriedly, he was on his way through the hallway when Tana Sato called him back and handed him her husband's spare ready-bag of instruments and drugs. Mumbling his thanks, he ran out of the house, down the drive, and onto the road, heading towards the crossroads.

Five hundred meters from the surging glare the heat was intense, attacking his exposed flesh. Vegetation was withering visibly, road lights were shattered, and trees lay in splintered fragments across the foothpath. The quality of the light in the heart of the conflagration seared his eyeballs. He put on a pair of dark glasses, and, slackening his pace to a brisk walk, he went on.

At a hundred and fifty meters the heat made further advances impossible. His clothes, unsuitably thin, began to smell singed. He backed a few paces, and stood looking at the inferno. One thing was certain; everyone in the village of Tamah was totally incinerated. There could be no survivors. Baba, along with her bed, and her barful of bottles, was nothing more than a few fragments of hot ash. "Not a good woman," Sato had said. Perhaps not, but she had given him some sympathy, some comfort in his useless loneliness that even Mia could not provide. One thing certain, she would not be drumming her heels in the small of his back again. . . .

He was still staring at the heart of the fire. What could have caused it? A fireball, a metor? A missile from an orbiting satellite? As far as he knew, Kepler had no such weapons, they had no need. . . .

His eyes drifted to the edge of the fire, where the ravening flames met unconsumed grass and turf. Unconsumed? As he watched the creeping edge of the fire it seemed that the earth, the very soil itself, was melting and burning away.

With the heat on his face, he found that he was shivering.

The sound of an approaching engine brought him back to reality. It was a fire float, squat, red, buglike, with a top-sprouting of nozzles. It surged and sank to a halt, spilling heat-suited men who connected light hoses to the nozzles and, each behind his shield, began to advance on the bubbling rim of the hell-hole, shooting streams of foam spray in the direction of the conflagration.

One man whose heat-suit bore an officer's stars approached Piet. "You see this?"

Piet felt a sudden thud of caution. "I . . . I came to see what it was."

"When did it start?"

Piet told him, and was interrupted after a couple of sentences by the arrival of two more fire floats. The officer broke away and went to confer with the new arrivals. The floats lifted again and took up station to encircle the fire, before disembarking men who followed the same drill as the first team. But as far as Piet could see the foam was making little impression. The fire was all-consuming, as if the disaster, whatever it was, had succeeded in setting up a slow chain reaction in hitherto nonradioactive matter.

The officer returned to Piet. "You live around here —see it all?"

"Yes." Suddenly Piet realized the particular difficulty he was in. This officer would want a statement . . .

"About what time did—?"

"Matsu!" someone shouted. "Have you got the temperature clock there?"

The officer questioning Piet turned to address the man who had called, and Piet took the opportunity to walk away. He had gone about fifty meters when he heard someone calling. He broke into a run, cursing his luck. There were no survivors on whom he could exercise his medical skill. The only result of his errand had been to attract the attention of the fire officer, who would surely get in touch with the police in order to trace such an important witness.

Kenji Sato was alone in the office of the hospital superintendent. Recognizing that he was unsteady, through anxiety and overwork, Mary Osawa had ordered him out of the delivery room, and he had accepted that order almost gratefully, content to leave the task in her more capable hands. In the meantime he had called Dan Shimaza, Yoko's mining-engineer husband in western Minashu, and Shimaza was already on his way to Main City by the first available jet flight. And now there was nothing to do but wait . . . his hands trembling, resisting with difficulty the urge to take a heavy shot of methidine.

Dragging himself from his chair, he walked across to the wall screen and switched on just in time to catch the first newscast of the day.

". . . at the crossroads of a small village named Tamah, about ten kilometers east of Main City." The newsreader's voice went on describing, as the screen showed the devastated area in shocking detail. ". . . said that the topsoil is now burned down a matter of ten to fifteen centimeters. . . ." The screen showed a black, flattened depression, with a few irregularities at the center which had once been the houses and other buildings at the crossroads. ". . . combined fire forces managed to stamp out the conflagration after a desperate eight-hour fight, and scientists are now examining the area in an attempt to discover the cause of the disaster. In this respect, police and fire authorities would like to interview a tall man who appeared to be of mixed Asiatic and Western parentage, and is believed to have been one of the first people on the scene after the occurrence of the outbreak. Casualties are difficult to assess at this time, but it is believed that over a hundred and fifty people living in the area of the Tamah crossroads must have perished. . . ."

His face rigid with shock, Kenji Sato switched off the TV screen and hurried to the desk vidphone.

He sagged with relief when his wife's face appeared in the small screen. "The Lord Buddha be praised—you are all right, Tana?"

"Yes, Kenji. We were far enough from the center of the disaster to suffer nothing more than a few damaged windows," she reassured him.

He remembered the tall Eurasian, whom the TV announcer had mentioned. "And our visitors?"

"They are also unharmed," said Tana. "Don't worry about us. How is Yoko? Is there any news yet?"

"Not yet, my love. I will call you again as soon as I have anything to tell." He hesitated. "You're sure you're all right? I could come, if you need me. There's little I can do here, at the moment."

"No—you must stay there near Yoko. She needs your strength by her at this time. Goodbye, Kenji."

"Goodbye. . . ." Sato switched off the vidphone, and sat staring at its blank screen. *My strength!* How can Tana go on believing in my strength when at this time I am less than useless? Unable to help Tana, or Yoko, impotent, useless and old. He thought of Huygens, who was there at the house with Tana—would he be of any help in an emergency?

He started, as the intercom on the desk buzzed, then pressed a button.

Mary Osawa said: "Kenji-san, come now."

She was waiting in the delivery room, alone with Yoko. The girl was sleeping, her face very pale, breathing lightly as the father hurried to the bedside. "Sedation?"

"I thought it best. Her time was not easy." Mary Osawa's voice was flat, emotionless.

He looked up. Her round, homely face was a stone mask, only the eyes were alive, filled with pain.

"The baby?"

She pointed in silence to a door.

He closed his eyes for a moment in silent prayer, then hurried through the door.

The child lay in the warm, transparent case of the incubator. Its nakedness was a pink, alien obscenity of distorted limbs and grotesquely misshapen trunk. Only the face, apart from the multiple-faceted, insectlike eyes, was minimally human.

"God! Where is our sin?" Kenji Sato slumped to his knees, covering his face with his hands in an attempt to shut out the dreadful image. But it remained with him.

At last he became aware of a touch on his shoulder. "Kenji," said Mary Osawa. "You must save your strength for Yoko. When she awakes, she will need you more than ever before."

Again this reference to his strength. How could they have—still maintain such faith in—a quality that he could no longer believe in himself? A man who no longer had honor could not have strength. And a man who had failed, as he had failed, could not have honor. . . .

"Kenji-san." Again, the insistent voice of Mary Osawa.

He allowed himself to be drawn to his feet, then, with a supreme effort of will, he removed his hands from in front of his eyes, and forced himself to look once again on the thing that was his grandchild.

This time his reaction was a new one, born of rage against fate and the knowledge of what he must do. Lifting the cover of the incubator, he reached down and, with the fingers of his right hand, firmly closed the nose and the mouth of the tiny monster.

The task completed, he wrapped the corpse in a sheet. There was no need of words between the two of them, they both knew what had to be done. Mary Osawa held the door open for him, and then accompanied him as he carried the small burden to the hospital incinerator.

Afterwards, the two of them returned to Mary Osawa's office.

"What will we do now, Kenji?" she asked, making him realize that by his positive action he had once more re-established his position as her superior, as the decision-maker. It was a position that he had no real desire to resume, because his mind was still preoccupied by the private problems presented by this new situation—the prospect of meeting Yoko's enquiring eyes when she recovered from the sedative, of meeting her eyes, and explaining to her that he had failed her.

And then there was Tana. Faithful, loving Tana, who had trusted in him, relied on him completely to save their daughter from a second horror. Tana, who was even now awaiting his vidphone call, who had talked only last night of the day soon to come when they would plant together the second *sakura* tree by the main entrance of their house, signifying the birth of their grandchild. That tree would never be planted now, because what had happened here today proved beyond doubt that the seed on which its planting depended, Yoko's seed, was irrevocably tainted.

"I must go to President Kido," Sato said. "And tell him that I have failed."

"No, Kenji-san," Mary Osawa objected. "You could not possibly have known, or even guessed."

He looked at her sadly, wishing that he could find comfort in her excuses for him. "I think that all along, even when I was reassuring Yoko that her second baby would be normal, somehow I knew that I was lying."

"That is impossible!" Mary Osawa's voice took on a touch of sharpness. "In all the records we have of Johannsen's disease, there has never before been a case of a woman, once she is free of infection, giving birth to a second malformed child. The evidence is there in the files, and it cannot be discounted."

"Mary," he said gently. "I made the fatal mistake of assuming, on the basis of the accompanying syndrome, that what we were dealing with here was a variety of the common Johannsen's disease virus. This is not the case, as has been demonstrated by today's tragedy. The Johannsen's virus does indeed cause the birth of malformed children, through its action on the growing fetus in the womb, but what we are dealing with here is something much more far-reaching in its effects; a virus which has the power to attack and modify the genetic structure of the human reproductive cells."

Mary Osawa's heavy body seemed to shrivel inside her white coverall as she stared at her chief. "What you're saying is that no woman who has suffered from the effects of this particular virus can ever again bear normal human children?"

"There is no other possible conclusion," agreed Sato. "And further, if the disease continues to spread as it is doing at the moment, this must mean that the time will soon come when there is no longer *any* woman on Kepler III capable of bearing a normal human child."

"Is there nothing we can do?"

"There may be, if I can persuade President Kido to agree with me," Sato said. "I have reason to believe that with the help of the Corps doctors, and the resources of *Venturer Twelve,* it may still be possible to save our people. There is unlikely to be any way of reversing the genetic effects of the disease on those who have suffered from it already—but if we can stamp it out, there is at least a chance that we shall be able to save those who have not yet been attacked."

"And if President Kido refuses to agree?" asked Mary Osawa.

Sato looked at her steadily, his ravaged face drained of blood, of life itself. "Then our colony is doomed," he said.

Charles Magnus did not share Commander Bruce's dislike of Keplerian food. Carefully schooled in Japanese gastronomy by the efficient Ichiwara, he was able to acquit himself with some distinction during the lunch with President Kido. Wielding his *hashi* with the aplomb of an expert, he moved daintily as a bee among the three tables of dishes placed before him, finding the task as absorbing as playing a five-keyboard organ.

Kido was clearly a man with an enormous appetite both for food and power. Afterwards, when the debris of the meal had been removed, and small pots of pale green tea had been served by self-effacing kimono-clad female members of his host's household, Magnus relaxed for a while on a silken couch, listening with some alarm to the rumblings of the presidential belly. At last, judging that a reasonable time had elapsed, he allowed himself, with suitable circumlocution, to approach the subject which had been the true purpose of his visit.

Kido listened attentively, his constant smile marred only occasionally by an unruly explosion of flatulence. "My dear Mr. Magnus, you did right to bring this matter to my attention. I have no detailed knowledge of the operation, of course, beyond the awareness that the matter was delegated to my Minister of Health, Doctor Sato. However, I think that I can understand what has happened. As your Mr. Ichiwara has no doubt explained to you already, we are by nature a tidy race, and an industrious one. In most situations these attributes would be looked upon as virtues, but there are occasions when they can prove an embarrassment. Among the officers of my government, Doctor Sato is perhaps one of the most zealous and industrious; a truly good man, and a fine physician, but a man also who is preoccupied to the point of obsession by a desire for order and tidiness. I have myself found it necessary on several occasions to beg him to spare himself some of the burdens which he insists on undertaking. . . ."

Magnus listened, sipping his tea quietly. To his mind, practiced in diplomatic maneuvers, it was all too obvious that the "excellent" Doctor Sato was a sacrificial goat being readied for the knife.

"It seems quite clear to me," continued Kido, "that although the request was for a random sample of the Keplerian population, Doctor Sato must have taken it upon himself to order some kind of preselection—not out of any desire to present a false picture, of that I am sure, but rather in a misguided attempt to assist your medical men in their investigations. Knowing Doctor Sato as I do, I can quite clearly see that the very idea of a "random" sample would be abhorrent to him. I have no doubt that you will find upon examination of the record cards concerned that he has been at great pains to present you with a carefully distributed cross-section in all respects."

Magnus nodded. "Yes, this is indeed the case. But Lieutenant Maseba insists, quite rightly, that if it is to have any validity at all, an investigation of this nature must be based on a completely random sample of the population. Further, I would add that this point was made quite clear in my original directive."

President Kido shook his head penitently. "My dear Mr. Magnus, I can only offer you my sincere apologies, and assure you that I will get in touch with Doctor Sato immediately and have the mistake rectified. Perhaps the best way of doing this would be for him to arrange with his records department that all cards should be made available to Lieutenant Maseba, so that he can make his own selection?"

"That seems like a good idea," agreed Magnus.

"The only drawback is that, after he has made such a selection, it will take some time to arrange for the subjects concerned to be made available for examination," Kido pointed out.

"We can wait, Mr. President," Magnus said smoothly.

As he listened to the terrible intelligence brought to him by Doctor Sato, Kido's mind was already planning and discarding, considering probabilities coolly, unhampered by anything but practical considerations. Sato, he was already aware, was an idealist, predictable, well-meaning. But then Sato could afford such luxuries—a second-generation professional man, who had never known hunger and want, who had been sheltered from all the invaluable formative influences which had forged the character of Kido. Sato could talk, giving way to unseemly emotion, as he spoke of the second monster born to his unfortunate daughter, could indulge in breast-beating self-condemnation of his own mistakes . . . but in the last resort it must be the man who kept his head, who chose unemotionally between the various courses of action who survived . . .

and Kido was in no doubt about the identity of that man.

On the face of it, there seemed a possibility that a disclosure of this kind might well cause Magnus to change his mind about granting independence to Kepler III, despite his professed favorable opinion. But even if that happened, there seemed no reason why the situation could not be handled to Kido's advantage—he had, after all, managed very well as president of the colonial government for the last nine years. The people were more interested in independence from a symbolic point of view than any practical advantage. True, there were likely to be certain economic benefits accruing from a freely negotiated transport contract with the corporation, and the standard of life for the average Keplerian could be expected to rise—but for Shanon Kido the matter was purely an academic one, provided he remained in power—and of his ability to maintain this condition he had little doubt.

"My dear Sato, calm yourself," he said. "This whole affair is unfortunate—but we shall, with careful deliberation, find a way out."

Sato, haunted eyes deep-set in his lined, bony face, raised his hands in despair. "The Lord Buddha grant that you are right, Mr. President—but at the moment I can see nothing ahead but the extinction of all our hopes, all our dreams. It has been said, truly, that the future of a planet lies in its children—if the very seed of our loins is poisoned, then what future can there be?"

"But surely that only applies to those people who have suffered from Johannsen's disease," Kido said. "Was it not you who urged that with the help of the Corps medical staff from *Venturer Twelve* the disease could be completely eradicated from our planet within a few months?"

"That still remains true," Sato said. "But those measures will do nothing to reverse the genetic effects of the disease on the reproductive cells of those who have already been infected. Such people can produce nothing but monstrous mutations of the kind with which we are already familiar."

Kido spread his hands. "Then they must not be allowed to breed. A simple program of selective sterilization . . ."

"But it is a terrible step to take," protested Sato. "To rob perhaps twenty percent of our adult population of their God-given power to procreate . . ."

"Have you any other alternative to offer?"

"Well, no . . . but—"

"Then that is what must be done," said Kido. "It will be necessary to throw ourselves on the mercy of Magnus, to explain the entire situation to him, and tell him the practical steps we intend to take. In the face of such sacrifice, he could hardly refuse to grant us his full cooperation."

"Even though we have deliberately deceived him?" said Sato.

"Yes, even that, if the circumstances of the deception are made sufficiently clear," Kido said. "Charles Magnus is a just man."

After the vidphone call was finished, Tana Sato went straight back to the guest room, where Mia and Piet Huygens were waiting.

"That was the hospital," she said.

"News of Yoko's baby?" Mia said.

Tana frowned. "No—nothing. Apparently there's been some delay, and Kenji has decided it would be best if I were there after all. I can't understand why he didn't call me himself . . ."

"Perhaps he is helping with the delivery," suggested Piet, comfortingly.

"Yes . . . I suppose that's it," said Tana, nodding. "Anyway, I shan't have to drive myself. They're sending a fast hopper over from the hospital to take me right there."

"Is there anything I can do?" Mia asked, beginning to rise.

"No, no, my dear child," Tana said. She smiled at the young couple. "Just take care of each other while I'm away. And keep indoors. Remember the police are still searching."

Piet nodded. "We'll do that, Tana . . . on one condition . . ."

"Condition?"

"That you promise to call us the very moment Yoko's baby is born," he said, gently.

"Surely she should have been back by now, or at least have called us and told us what is happening?" said Mia, on the second morning following Tana's departure for the hospital.

"We shall hear, all in good time," Piet said, putting on his clothes. "Now you just stay right where you are, and I'll fix you something. What'll it be—eggs?"

She shook her head, smiling sleepily. "Do you know what I'd *really* like?" she said, raising herself on one elbow. "A couple of slices of that rock-hard, protein-enriched, soy-bread toast smeared with algae-processed margarine and flavor-bud-tickling yeast concentrate, like we used to get in the crew mess back on *Vee Twelve.*"

"Ugh!" Piet grimaced. "You have a pretty gruesome taste in dainties."

"Maybe it's not me," she pointed out. "Young Piet is making his presence felt physically these days; could be he's begun dictating the menu as well."

"In that case, you can tell his lordship he's having eggs, whether he likes it or not," Piet said. "Time to start throwing his weight about when he can talk for himself." He walked through to the kitchen, flipped on the TV for the morning news, and began to prepare breakfast. Supplies were getting low, he reflected, as he cracked the last three eggs into a bowl. If Tana didn't get back soon, he would have to go out on a grocery-buying expedition, despite the risk. But maybe . . .

His train of thought broke off as the voice of the TV news reader broke through.

". . . representatives of all media were called to the presidential palace for an emergency press conference at twenty-seven hundred hours last night. After a brief introduction by his public relations officer, President Kido made a statement . . ."

The screen dissolved to a close shot of the round, Buddalike features of the president.

"My friends, I have called you here at this last hour to inform you of a matter of the gravest import. You all know that it has been my policy, and that of your government, to cooperate to the fullest extent with the Explorations Division officer in charge of the independence investigation. It is now my distasteful duty to tell you that contrary to all my directives a serious breach of that cooperation has been made by a high-ranking and trusted official of your government. Mr. Magnus has already been informed of the complete nature of this breach and he will no doubt be making a statement himself when he has had time to consider its implications fully. We can only hope that he will in his wisdom refrain from punishing us all for the ill-considered actions of the person responsible. In the meantime, you, the people, have the right to know the facts which have been brought to my notice.

"As you all know, the independence investigation is a complex operation, covering all aspects of our existence here on Kepler III. In all departments, save one, your ministers have cooperated willingly and frankly with the Explorations Division investigators, and that exception, which has been brought to my notice, is in the important sector of public health . . ."

Abandoning his task, Piet moved across the kitchen and turned up the volume as the president continued.

"For reasons best known to himself, Doctor Sato, your Minister of Health, has withheld information and made false statements to the independence investigation team. In particular, he has deliberately concealed the facts about the incidence in our population of an infectious illness known as Johannsen's disease. While this disease is not serious in itself, there are certain unpleasant side effects when it is contracted by women in the state of pregnancy, and this has, as many of you may know already, resulted in an increase in the number of still and malformed births. However, there is no need to be alarmed about this situation—I am assured that the Corps doctors aboard *Venturer Twelve* will be able to wipe out the disease completely within a very short time, because they have at their disposal all the necessary drugs and serums required for such an operation.

"Even so, I would be failing in my duty if I were to minimize the gravity of the possible effects of these revelations on the outcome of the independence investigations—it may well be that Doctor Sato's misguided actions will be the cause of our being denied that liberty for which we have worked so many years."

The president raised his hand dramatically to quell the angry murmurs growing around him. "Please, my friends, I beg you to remember that Mr. Magnus has shown sympathy and understanding towards our aspirations every since he has been on our planet, and that there is every likelihood that he will continue to do so. As for Doctor Sato, who is not here to defend his actions, I can only say that during my years of association with him, I have always considered him a sincere, hard-working government servant, zealous to the point of fanaticism in his pursuit of what he considered to be the common good. It may have been this fanaticism which led him, in addition to the falsification of vital records, to take the dreadful step of personally destroying those unfortunate creatures born of mothers who had suffered from Johannsen's disease during pregnancy, which were being cared for in an Intensive Care Unit near the northern mountains. Whatever the reason for this action, I beg of you, do not condemn Kenji Sato as a mass-murderer, but rather think of the good things that he has done in the service of our people. And now, my friends . . ."

Bitter disgust filling his mouth like bile, Piet switched down the sound and turned deliberately away from the wall screen. It was quite clear to him that Sato, wherever he was, had been made the scapegoat in a situation that threatened to get out of control. He himself had heard from Sato, in this very house, the facts of the case—the truth that Sato himself was worried about the situation, but had withheld the information about the incidence of Johannsen's disease from the investigating team on the direct orders of President Kido himself. Sato would say these things, when he appeared to defend himself, no doubt—or would he? In some respects Kido's assessment of Sato's character had been a true one—the good doctor was indeed possessed of a certain kind of stubborn fanaticism. If he came to the conclusion that he might harm the cause of his people by defending himself, then he would be just as likely to allow himself to be sacrificed as a scapegoat without a murmur of protest.

"You've been a long time, love." Mia, a green silk robe thrown over her shoulders, appeared in the doorway of the kitchen.

"I'm sorry, Mia," he said, turning to meet her. "There was a presidential statement on . . ."

The expression on Mia's face stopped him in mid-sentence. She stared past him, looking at the TV screen, one small fist balled and crammed tight against her mouth.

He turned to see the cause of her horror, and found himself looking directly into a close-up shot of the dead faces of Kenji and Tana Sato. The two white-robed bodies lay side by side on a stone slab, and as Piet moved across and turned up the sound, the news reader's voice was saying: ". . . at the Akuno Temple, in an inner chamber, where the Minister and his dutiful wife committed hara-kiri during the early hours of this morning. Doctor Sato, for many years a respected member of the government service, was named in a statement last night by President Kido as . . ."

"Kenji-san and Tana, both dead. Oh, Piet, what can it mean?" sobbed Mia, as he helped her from the kitchen back to their room.

"For us, it means that we must leave here at once," he said. "Tana's car is in the garage. We must take it and get as far away as we can, as quickly as possible."

As the picture on the TV screen dwindled to a white dot and then disappeared, Charles Magnus turned to Ichiwara.

"Hara-kiri?"

Ichiwara's face was solemn. "Such a course would, under the circumstances, be quite a logical one for the unfortunate Doctor Sato. He has failed, and has been shown publicly to have done so."

Tom Bruce stopped in the act of lighting a long, thin cigarillo, and grunted: "The old escape clause."

Ichiwara's eyes moved sharply behind his pebble-thick glasses. "With respect, Commander, not altogether so simple. Hara-kiri, unlike your Western concept of suicide, is not usually considered as a way of evading one's responsibilities. It is a positive, rather than a negative, gesture. There are times when a man is placed in such a situation that there is no other honorable course open to him."

George Maseba massaged one lean cheek with the tips of his delicate surgeon's fingers. "You're suggesting that this could be some form of protest?"

"Against what, for God's sake?" snorted Bruce.

Ichiwara raised his shoulders in a very un-Oriental shrug. "One can only guess at this stage, but President Kido is a very devious man, that much is certain."

"And Sato was, without doubt, a man under considerable stress—very near to breaking point," said Maseba. "It's quite clear now that he must have engineered the preselection of the random sample expressly in order to conceal the facts about the incidence of Johannsen's disease—but I find it difficult to believe that he could have undertaken such a serious course of deception completely on his own initiative. On the other hand, if he were acting on orders from above . . ."

"You're suggesting that Kido knew all along about the deception?" said Magnus.

"I'll buy that," cut in Bruce. "That Kido is the smoothest slug I ever met, even for a politician."

Magnus nodded thoughtfully. "I must say I'm inclined to agree with you there, Commander."

"Well, in that case, you're surely not going to let him get away with it, are you?" Bruce said. "It looks very much to me as though Sato is nothing more than a scapegoat."

"There may be something in what you say, Commander, but one must also take into account the stakes involved," Magnus said. "Kido is not a medical man, and he may well have been led by Sato to believe that the existence of this disease on Kepler would constitute a barrier to the granting of independence."

"And it doesn't?" said Bruce.

"Well, that depends on Lieutenant Maseba," Magnus

said. "But if the outbreak can be stamped out within a reasonable time, I would be very loathe to let it stand in the way of a satisfactory conclusion to the independence investigation." He looked towards the medic.

Maseba frowned. "I don't want to be pushed into making a snap judgment on a matter as important as this. I'll have to check with stores, but I doubt if we shall have sufficient supplies of a suitable attenuated virus to immunize more than a tenth of the Keplerian population—and this has to be a hundred percent operation to be certain of success."

"Which means?"

"Well, we can hardly walk down to the corner drug store and buy the rest of what we need, can we?" said Maseba. "On the other hand, if the Keplerian pharmaceutical industry is in any kind of shape, it is possible that we could make arrangements to have further supplies cultivated. Always supposing, of course, that they would be prepared to cooperate."

"I don't think you need have any doubts about that," Magnus assured him. "Assuming full cooperation and adequate laboratory facilities, how long would it take to produce the quantities necessary and to carry out your immunization program?"

Maseba made a rapid calculation. "Two . . . three months, providing everything goes without a hitch . . . which it hardly ever does, I might add."

Bruce glowered as he saw his provisional schedule once more shot to hell.

Piet had decided to head for Hukayan, the city in the northeastern corner of the continent. The main thing initially was to put as much distance as possible between them and any connection with Doctor Sato. In a new city they would be strangers, but with their increased knowledge of Keplerian ways they would soon be accepted and he would be able to get some kind of job. In the meantime they had sufficient money for food and lodging for several weeks.

Once they had left the fertile plain of Main City province the country became much wilder, with crags and chasms torn from gray volcanic rock by ancient upheavals in the cooling crust of the planet. Vegetation was sparse and cactuslike. The only sign of man's influence was the great transcontinental highway. Built eight decades previously at tremendous cost, improved air transport using the anti-grav principle had now rendered the road obsolete, and in places it was being gradually reclaimed as part of the wilderness by rockfalls. However, it was still passable, and from the point of view of Piet and Mia the fact that they met only one other vehicle was a point in favor of this method of transport. The owner of the battered ground truck, a tattered man, equally as decrepit as his means of transport, passed them by with a cheery wave, and Piet guessed from the nature of the assorted gear piled in the back of the vehicle that he was some kind of prospector.

It was early afternoon when, having covered some 250 kilometers, Piet decided to stop at a parking place where the highway hugged the side of a hill in a long, outward-veering curve, giving a fine view of a valley beyond, the lushness of which showed that the character of the land had changed once again. After the bleakness of the landscape through which they had been passing for the past three hours it was reassuring to view the patchwork of farmlands which lay between them and the small town of Nisuno.

Mia clapped her hands. "Oh, how lovely! Let's have a picnic right here. I'm hungry."

Piet grinned. "Both of you." He pulled onto the parking place and dived into the back of the car for the food basket, while Mia got out and walked towards the edge of the steep slope. The basket had jammed some-how against the back of a seat, and he had to kneel on the seat to get it out. Eventually, heaving it up, he placed it down beside him and looked across towards where he had last seen Mia.

She was not there.

For a moment he thought nothing of it; then with a whimper of fear, he leaped from the car, the door crashing behind him. His feet rattled on the rocky debris as he dashed to the edge and looked down.

The slope was, maybe, sixty degrees at its steepest, with stunted bushes and outcrops of rock. Twenty meters down, buttressed by a rock, Mia lay with arms outspread, her eyes closed and her swollen belly an awful reminder of the complications which could result from such an accident.

Should we not sound them,
Assume they are there, and call into the black?
But we have—and no one answers back.
There's this conclusion then, that if they hear,
They're saying nothing. More than this,
Maybe they don't have to say a word,
Maybe they can just listen, and so learn
All they want.
  Are you shivering?

Kilroy: I. Kavanin

Jiro Osuragi, the local doctor in Nisuno, was a small, gray-haired man in his late fifties. Quietly matter-of-fact in his attitude, he took in the situation at a glance, and Mia was soon installed in a private ward of the small local clinic.

At first he seemed inclined to reject Piet's claim to

be a doctor, but as, on Piet's insistence, they examined the patient together, he was gradually convinced. Her injuries were fortunately minor, amounting to nothing more than a suspected cracked rib, multiple bruises of the legs and a slight concussion.

She recovered consciousness. "Oh, Piet, love, I'm an old silly. I leaned on that boulder and it just rolled away—and I rolled with it. Am I . . . ooh!" Her hand moved upwards towards the rib.

"You'll live," Piet said, smiling his reassurance. "But just scare me like that once more and I'll sue for divorce. My nerves won't stand it."

He had just finished attending to the cracked rib and dressed her abrasions when she had the first contraction.

"Piet, love, I think. . . ." She gritted her teeth against the pain.

"Don't try to talk," he said. "You're in a safe place, with two doctors in attendance. Everything is going to be all right."

Leaving her for a moment, he went outside the ward to confer with Doctor Osuragi on preparations for the delivery. When he came back she was lying still, her face screwed up with anxiety.

"Am I going to be all right?"

"Of course," he reassured her.

"How long?"

"I wouldn't be surprised if you managed it in three hours."

She shuddered and stiffened as a second contraction hit her. "Ooh—there it goes again," she gasped.

"Nothing to worry about." He saw that she was tense, and determined to give her something to relax her. "You know, Mia, there were times when—" he smiled broadly at her—"when I thought maybe you didn't need me much. It's good in a way to be quite sure again that you do."

"You thought I didn't—oh, Piet, how could you?"

"Well, never mind. I know you do now."

She gave a little shudder, and a gasp. "Oh . . . what was that?"

"You're doing fine. Cervical dilation beginning." He cleaned up, and Osuragi brought in the rest of the hardware he needed for the delivery, excusing himself afterwards to attend to other patients, now that he was confident that Mia was in capable hands.

After the doctor had gone, Piet said: "Now, let's get this trembling done with, shall we? A little jab, and then you'll feel all warm and cozy, and we can talk and squeeze, and talk and squeeze together."

Some time later, he said: "You're presenting fine."

A dozy giggle. "I'm what?"

"Presenting. He's in the right position. Exactly."

"A doctor's son, naturally."

"Like the tide coming in, Mia."

"What?"

"A little further each time, love, and he goes back a little."

He was so occupied with her needs that he mentally glimpsed only in the tiniest flashes who he was, and what he was—a man of Earth who had deserted his companions with a woman who had done the same. But she—she was now in her finest moment. His beloved Mia, strained, messy, utterly dependent on him, and he loved her more deeply than ever before. . . .

It was odd. Sometimes he saw himself doing a text-book job of delivery, sometimes as the loving husband who was miraculously able to do this important thing for his wife, and at others he saw himself as a man trapped by elemental forces, trapped by the very act that he had regarded as an exciting sport from his early teens—copulation.

She slid her hand down her belly. "Hey—what happened here?"

"What do you expect, girl? I shaved you."

She giggled again, and then her face twisted. When the spasm was past she relaxed again, and said: "I can't remember that."

And so it went on. The doctor was satisfied with his patient's progress. He could hear the textbook in his head . . . extension round subpubic arch begun . . . forward movement of the head satisfactory . . . time to move her left lateral, buttocks over edge . . . she was so light to him . . . and the first sight of the top of the little head, with the birth canal a tight ring. . . .

She was in a gentle, painless haze, but the husband thought in agony, God, what a terrible thing to be woman! and refused to be comforted by the assurances of the doctor. . . .

And then, with the next contraction, the confidence of the doctor too was shattered, as he saw that, easy though the birth might be, that which was being born was an offense to humanity.

She had a small shivering attack after the baby was out, but it soon passed. She was deeper in her hazy sleep, and he attended to her carefully. No tearing, blood clot out, cleaned and comfortable.

The noise he kept hearing was the grinding of his own teeth, as he did what was necessary. He felt the tears start at the thought that when she awoke she would want to hold her baby. . . .

He steeled himself to look again on what she had borne, trying to maintain the calm of the impartial doctor as he stared at the awful thing that had sprung from his seed.

Mia was not infected with Johannsen's disease, could not have been, as far as he knew. And himself—was he, perhaps, responsible?

Or was it perhaps that Sato had been completely wrong about the connection between Johannsen's disease and the monstrous births on Kepler III? Piet had no way of knowing it, but the ugly, short-legged, thick-bodied, four-armed thing which lay pink and quivering before him was the same kind of creature to which the unhappy Yoko had given birth.

Then, as he looked, it came to Piet what this thing really was. And with that knowledge, he knew quite clearly what he had to do. To him, with his medical training not long behind him, the hideous truth was apparent, and that truth must be told, whatever the cost.

Mia . . . there could be no question of moving her for the time being. She would have to remain here under the care of Doctor Osuragi while *he* did what he must.

Killing the nonhuman thing was not difficult. He no longer looked on it as part of himself or Mia.

She was still sleeping when he wrapped the body in a plastic sheet, and put it in a bag. He looked at her for a moment, then hurried out with his burden to the car.

Within five minutes he was out of the fertile valley, driving at top speed along the highway south, through the bleak, volcanic landscape. And he found himself wondering which was the more important; the call of duty that he, Piet Huygens, deserter, was obeying by returning in this way—or the escape that he, Piet Huygens, coward, was making from the questioning eyes of Mia when she awoke and asked for her baby. Perhaps it was neither, he reflected, perhaps what he was really obeying was a masochistic need to be punished for the crime he had committed in the name of love, because he was going to be punished, wanted it, and deserved it, and wanted to deserve it.

And Mia? He would probably never see her again, and perhaps it was best that way. . . .

He drove on, a bloody sun sagging into the primitive horizon on his left, staining the sky of Kepler III with its dreadful omen of horror as yet unrealized. . . .

Commander Bruce was jolted awake by the urgent voice issuing from the loudspeaker at his bedside. He sat up, automatically thumbing the "send" button. "Do you know I've been in this bed only two hours?"

"I'm sorry, sir, but I think you ought to come to the duty officer's room right away." Lee Ching's voice was firm.

"You *think*, Lieutenant?"

"I can't say any more over the intercom," said Lee Ching. "But this is an emergency." He broke contact.

Emergency . . . Bruce clawed out of bed, reaching for his zip suit, muttering to himself: "Emergency . . . I'll have his balls for gyros if it's anything less than an AAA distress. . . ."

By the time he reached the duty officer's room he was fully awake, the internal grumbling quieted, but what he found there puzzled him nevertheless. Lee Ching was standing by the desk, facing a man in the clothes of a Keplerian civilian. On the desk was a bundled zip bag, the presence of which brought about a sudden resurgence of Bruce's anger. If Lee Ching had got him out of bed to deal with a case of petty pilfering from ship's stores by some wretched civilian worker. . . .

This train of thought was broken off abruptly as *both* men saluted. Acknowledging curtly, Bruce walked round the desk and turned to face the prisoner; a black-haired man with the eyes of an Asiatic, who was taller than the average Keplerian by about thirty centimeters.

"It's Lieutenant Huygens, sir," explained Lee Ching. "He insisted that he had to see you personally."

It was so long since Bruce had seen the defecting medical officer, and the man's appearance was so different, that he had difficulty in squaring the situation up in his mind. Yes . . . it was Huygens, but the changes in this man were deeper than the mere cosmetic touches of coloring and eye-shape.

"All right, Huygens. So you've seen me. You've got yourself my undivided, personal attention." Bruce's voice was a quiet whiplash. "But before you say anything, anything at all, I'd advise you to think carefully." To Lee Ching, he said: "Get Maseba."

"Sir . . . my reasons . . ."

"Tell them to the court martial."

"But, sir . . ."

"You snivelling, undisciplined son of a bitch! Do you imagine that I'm interested in hearing your reasons?"

"Sir, I didn't come back just to give myself up . . ."

Bruce's green eyes were hard as slate. "I don't want to hear it, Huygens. You're under close arrest, as of now, and when we're back in space you'll be courtmartialed. Not here, on Kepler, where you might attract some misguided sympathy. And when we get back to Earth, you'll get a dishonorable discharge and then serve out your sentence in a civilian jail. I loathe and detest you for what you've done to the Corps, Huygens, and you're never going to be allowed to forget that crime . . ."

"Commander Bruce . . . sir!" It was a cry for help, but Bruce was too preoccupied with his righteous rage to recognize it as such.

Maseba came into the room, nodded to Lee, and stood listening.

Bruce continued, his voice harsh, uncompromising. "There are some people in this crew who have made excuses for you, Huygens, but I'm not one of them. They've adduced various so-called reasons for what you did. But as far as I'm concerned the facts speak for themselves. You're a disgrace . . ."

"Sir! For God's sake!" Huygen's voice was a stran-

gled shout. "Listen to me! I didn't have to come back.
I could have stayed out there, and you would never
have found me. But I did come back, and you've got to
listen to me! Look at this!" Tension in the room increased, as he stepped forward and unzipped the bag.
Lee Ching moved to restrain him, then stopped as
Huygens removed the transparent plastic container and
held it up in full view. "Look, damn you! Mia—my
wife—*this is the thing she gave birth to!*"

Bruce looked at the terrible, unhuman shape, the
impetus of his rage faltering. "You mean your . . .
Mizuno? Maseba said that a Comp. Ab.—"

Piet cried out in anguish. "I wish to God she'd had
that Comp. Ab.! Anything, if she could have been
spared this. I wish we'd never. . . ." He swayed for a
moment, then choked back his sobs. "No, maybe I
don't, because if I hadn't seen this one, then none of
us would have been given the opportunity of seeing one
of these . . . things. Sato covered up the whole affair,
because he thought in his ignorance that they were due
to the effects of Johannsen's disease—because, well-
meaning fool that he was, he could see no further than
the goal of Keplerian independence."

Maseba was looking at the creature closely, his eyes
filled with alarm.

"But you recognize it, commander, don't you?"
Huygens continued. "You should know better than any
of us, if I remember my medical history. This is one of
the things which the Kilroys were trying to make when
they experimented with the colonists on Minos IV—
the rejects which you shot out of mercy, all that long
time ago, when I was just a little boy at school . . . the
ones they showed pictures of at the *Athena* inquiry.
We all know those pictures, those dissections, and what
they represent . . ."

"Gods of all the tribes defend us!" Maseba spoke
quietly; the brown-flecked whites of his eyes showing
boldly as he bent forward. He slipped his pink palms

under the specimen and lifted it out of Huygen's grasp.

Bruce said: "What are you talking about? Those things I found on Minos IV were produced by surgery on adult humans."

"That's right, they were," agreed Huygens, "but now the Kilroys must have gone a stage further. Using Johannsen's disease, which we already know to have an affinity for human reproductive cells, they have re-structured the virus, inserting specific episomes which are capable of altering the human genetic code and causing these creatures to be produced by human mothers. Kepler III is, in effect, an experimental farm."

Bruce looked towards Maseba. "This is possible?"

Maseba, still holding the terrible evidence in his hands, nodded. "Ruthless genetic engineering on a massive scale. Creatures of one species molded out of the living cells of another . . . for the Kilroys, yes, this would be possible."

"But for what reason . . . ?"

"Can we even begin to understand the motivation of a completely nonhuman race, with whom we have never made direct contact?"

Bruce's lean face was grave as he stared at the dread-ful thing in Maseba's hands. "We may be reaching the crisis point of that situation too," he said.

Maseba frowned. "Commander?"

"I was thinking," said Bruce. "Assuming that this theory of Kepler III being an experimental farm is correct—then surely the Kilroys will be along some time soon to see how their crop is coming along?"

Maseba's office was darkened, and quiet save for the small whirring of the cooling fan on the projector which was being operated by Leela De Witt. Apart from the two medics, there were four people present; Charles

Magnus, his assistant Ichiwara, Bruce, and Helen Lindstrom. Seated next to her commander she felt a prickling down her spine as she looked at the black paper-doll things on the screen and considered the idea of a war whose battleground was the microscopic genetic inheritance of the human race.

Maseba touched the screen with his light pointer. "Here you see the karotype of a normal human chromosome pattern. Using the Denver Classification System, the chromosomes are lined up by size and shape into seven groups of autosomes and two gonosomes, which determine the sex of the embryo. When a sperm fertilizes an ovum, each supplies half the forty-six chromosomes for the combination of cells that will grow into a baby. To give you some idea of the complexity of this process, I should add that each of these chromosomes contains up to one thousand two hundred and fifty genes, and each of these genes determines some factor, or combination of factors, in the makeup of the individual. Despite the eugenics laws, which as you know require persons intending to breed to submit themselves for genetic examination, et cetera, in a growth disorder like Mongolism, something goes wrong with the process of cell division in the embryo and such patients are found to have forty-seven chromosomes instead of the normal forty-six. Another common abnormality is concerned with the gonosomes, where instead of splitting into two neat rows of twenty-three each, an extra X or Y chromosome is left in one row. If the supernumerary is an X, the baby has an XXY pattern. It will grow into a sterile, asthenic 'male,' usually with some breast enlargement and mental retardation—the condition known as Klinefelter's syndrome. If the extra chromosome is a Y, then the baby gets an XYY pattern and is unquestionably male, but over-aggressive and potentially criminal. Right, Leela."

In response to Maseba's command, another picture appeared on the screen beneath the first one.

"Now," he continued, "the abnormalities I have mentioned so far are already well-known to us. They have no direct bearing on our present problem, except as an illustration of the terrible effects that may occur as a result of the tiniest rearrangement of genetic material. The karotype you now see beneath our original has been produced from the white blood cells of Mia Mizuno's child. In this case we see that, instead of the normal three pairs of autosomes in the fourth group, there are in fact four pairs; additional to this, instead of there being one pair of gonosomes, either XY or XX, that is male or female, there are two pairs, XX *and* XY. Thus, instead of the normal total of forty-six we have a being whose cell structure contains fifty chromosomes—the extra pair of autosomes in the fourth group, presumably governing the growth process which produces the physical abnormalities found in Mia's child, and the extra pair of gonosomes indicating that on maturity this creature would probably become a male/female creature capable of fulfilling either function in the breeding process."

Magnus asked, "Is it your opinion that this kind of chromosome structure could have been produced by the accidental processes of mutation?"

"It *could* have been," replied Maseba. "But the odds against that happening are extremely high. In the past, radical mutations in the human species have been, mercifully, rare, and in most cases nonviable. This creature, on the other hand, appears to me to have been extremely well equipped for survival and would, in its adult state, have been more than a match for the normal human being in the physical sense. Even so, I might have been prepared to concede the possibility of such an accident, had it not been for the karotype of this third tissue sample which Lieutenant De Witt is about to show you."

The third slide appeared on the screen beneath the other two, as Maseba continued: "You are all aware of the postulation made in the first instance by Lieutenant Huygens that the birth of such children to human women could be due to the effects of some unknown strain of Johannsen's disease which is capable of modifying the structure of human reproductive cells. Initially there seemed to me to be a certain inconsistency in this theory, because for this to have happened in the case of Mia Mizuno, it implied that she should have suffered at some time during her pregnancy from this particular disease—a form which, as far as we know, only exists on Kepler III. And, you will recall, Mia Mizuno's pregnancy began some months before we arrived on this planet.

"I have not yet had the opportunity to examine Crewwoman Mizuno, but I suspect that when I do so, I shall find that she has never, in fact, suffered from Johannsen's disease. Lieutenant Huygens, on the other hand, was for some period of time in a situation where he could quite easily have contracted the disease, working with the cadavers and in company with personnel who were potential carriers of the virus."

"The *Wangituru!*" exclaimed Bruce.

"Precisely," agreed Maseba. "The crew of the *Wangituru,* only a few weeks out from Kepler III, are clearly our carriers, and it must have been from one of them that Huygens contracted Johannsen's disease. The symptoms of the disease are comparatively mild, and Huygens dismissed them as unimportant at the time, treating himself, and omitting to report the matter to me. The results of that omission you now see on the screen before you in a karotype of reproductive cells taken from Huygens. This, as comparison will show you, exhibits the same modifications of chromosome structure as the second sample, that from the body of the monstrous child. Thus proving that this altered genetic structure, transmitted by the sperm of Huygens into the ovum of Mia Mizuno, was capable of changing her normal human chromosome pattern, and imposing on it the aberrations which resulted in her bearing this nonhuman creature."

"I take it that implies that this mutation is a dominant one?" said Magnus.

"That is something I can only be sure of when I have had the opportunity of examining the chromosome structure of a reasonable sample of Keplerian men and women, but I would be inclined to agree with you," Maseba said.

"And you are in no doubt about the connection between Johannsen's disease and this mutation?" said Bruce.

"This particular strain of Johannsen's disease virus," Maseba corrected him precisely. "The idea of a virus tailored for a particular purpose is not, of course, a new one. It has been known for over two centuries that viruses are the ultimate parasites, consisting of little more than a protein shell enclosing a core of hereditary material which is discharged into the cell attacked by the virus. Here we are dealing with a type of supervirus which possesses an in-built tropism towards human reproductive cells. Unlike other viruses, it does not destroy those cells which it attacks, but merges with them, modifying their structure in accordance with its own chromosome pattern. The insertion of episomes, genetic instructions, in this manner is not entirely unknown. Our own scientists have experimented with the method of plant breeding, and there have been a number of laboratory experiments with animal tissue. The truly frightening things about the present situation are the unavoidable conclusion that whoever produced modified Johannsen's virus must have done so with the conscious purpose of inducing mutation in human beings, and the fact that to perform such a feat they must be possessed of genetic-engineering techniques so far ahead of our own as to make them appear quite primitive."

Maseba switched on the light. His listeners remained

silent for several moments. Helen felt a cold fear deep down inside herself as she considered the implications of what he had said, and she guessed that the others must be experiencing something similar.

Tom Bruce was the first to break the silence. "The Kilroys." His voice was sharp-edged with loathing.

"Do you agree, Lieutenant Maseba?" said Magnus.

Maseba shrugged. "Well, let's put it this way. I can't think of any more likely explanation. The chances of such a virus with just such qualities arising naturally are so small as to be hardly worthy of consideration. Add to this the undoubted similarity of this birth to some types of surgically altered humans found by Commander Bruce on Minos IV, and there doesn't appear to be much doubt."

Magnus nodded. "Assuming that your analysis of the situation is correct—and I have no reason to suppose that it isn't—do you have any recommendations?"

Maseba frowned. "I have had very little time to consider . . ."

Magnus raised one hand. "My dear Lieutenant, I'm not asking you to commit yourself in any way, but as the person closest to this problem, who has a greater understanding of its complexity than any of us, I consider that even your off-the-cuff reflections may have considerable value."

"So long as it is quite understood that they are off-the-cuff," Maseba said, his expression easing slightly. "Well, before I start I must make it clear that whatever the solution to this situation may be, it isn't going to be produced overnight, so you, Mr. Magnus, and Commander Bruce, can forget about your schedules. For a start, we shall have to get on with the job of trying to develop some method of stamping out Johannsen's disease on Kepler III where, I suspect, it is endemic and fast growing towards epidemic proportions, despite the efforts of the late Doctor Sato and his staff. Just what direction they have been working in we don't know at present, but it will no doubt be possible now to arrange a closer liaison. Whatever they have been doing, it has clearly not been successful so far. For my part, assuming that I were allowed the necessary resources in skilled workers and time, I would mount a three-pronged attack, to explore the possibilities of (a) developing an attenuated strain of the virus, (b) attempting to produce a serum which might provide immunity, and (c) exploring the effects of antiviral agents of the Interferon type on this particular subject."

"That sounds like a good beginning," Magnus said approvingly. "Assuming all the necessary resources and time were made available to you, what would your next step be?"

"One which will require even greater resources than the first one, I'm afraid," said Maseba. "Here we are faced with a situation in which the usual sampling techniques will just not do. Every human being on Kepler III will have to be subjected to a complete eugenic analysis. Until that task has been completed, we have no way of telling just how widespread this Johannsen's-induced chromosome pattern is among the population."

"And when we do know—will there be any possible way of remedying the situation?"

"By a readjustment of each person's individual chromosome back to the normal human pattern?" Maseba smiled sadly. "I doubt if even the Kilroy genetic engineers could tackle that one."

Helen Lindstrom was conscious of a new fear as she considered the implications of Maseba's latest statement, a fear which, as a woman, she could not ignore. "If such readjustment is, as you suggest, impossible, what then would be your next step?"

The pain on Maseba's dark face made it evident that his own assessment of the situation was the same as her own. "Under those circumstances, the only possible way of ensuring that this aberrated chromosome pattern is not perpetuated will be to carry out an irrevocable sterilization of all human beings carrying the pattern. At the moment it is quite impossible to assess just how many people that is likely to involve—but I would guess that it would entail a significant fraction of the entire population of Kepler III."

A significant fraction. . . . Helen found herself attempting to contemplate just what the abstraction meant. The only way in which she could think of the problem was in terms of the personal suffering of Mia Mizuno and Piet Huygens, and to try to imagine such suffering multiplied by many thousands. It was an impossible task, which left her immersed in an overwhelming sadness that paralyzed all logical thought, so that apart from odd snatches the rest of the discussion failed to register on her mind at all.

When the session was at last over, she left Maseba's office immediately for the quiet, gray sanctuary of her own cabin, where she allowed herself the private emotional release of tears.

Now it was the time of waiting. Bruce was commander of *Venturer Twelve,* United Earth's newest and most powerful ship—in Corps terms he was "the man on the spot." Magnus was the Explorations Division officer—a man of tremendous power and intelligence, capable of being entrusted with the future of an entire planet, Kepler III. But in this extraordinary situation which must involve the entire future of the human race, neither could make the decisions required of them with complete confidence. In the past there had been differences between them, but for the time being at least they were agreed in this assessment of their limitations.

They sat together in the commander's office, awaiting a reply from Earth, Bruce drawing on one of his thin, dark cigars, sensing the nearness of a confrontation which he had awaited since that day on Minos IV long years before, and Magnus, apparently relaxed, leafing through his copy of the report which had been sent back to Earth.

The report, complex, all-inclusive, referring to the situation on Kepler III, with an appended list of recommended suggested action, had been transmitted by subetheric direct to Henry Fong, the president of United Earth, a message which, even taped, coded and accelerated for transmission, had run some twenty-five minutes. And now, some two hours later, they were still waiting.

Bruce crumpled the remains of his cigar in an ashtray and jabbed his forefinger at the button on the desk intercom.

"Communications."

"Maranne? Anything through yet?"

"No, commander."

"Not even an acknowledgment?"

"No, sir. I shall contact you direct, the moment we hear."

"Do that." Bruce broke the connection.

"Patience, commander." Magnus looked up from his reading. "We can hardly expect a snap decision from Fong in a question of this magnitude, and allowing for the half hour time lag you must remember he has had less than ninety minutes to study the report. Even then, I suspect he will not reply entirely on his own judgment —there will have to be consultation."

"Maybe so—but they could at least have acknowledged receipt," Bruce said.

"An oversight, possibly."

"Oversight, be damned! It's blasted inefficiency!" snapped Bruce. "I want to get *Vee Twelve* into space, where she can defend herself and Kepler III, should the situation arise. Here on Rokoa field she's a sitting duck for any Kilroy ship that appears."

"And has been for the last couple of months," Magnus pointed out mildly. "The situation hasn't changed in its essentials."

"Perhaps not, but our awareness of it has," Bruce said. "Sooner or later they're going to come back here, and when they do I want to be ready for them. The way I see it, every moment's delay increases the probability of a Kilroy ship arriving before we blast off."

"I fully appreciate your feelings, commander," Magnus said. "But you must be patient. One wrong move at this stage and we could have a planet-wide panic on our hands."

Bruce grunted, and lit another cigar. "So we sit here, with our pants down, waiting for instructions from Earth."

"We have no alternative."

"With no acknowledgment from Earth—that's what bothers me. Sub-etheric is new, we don't have sufficient experience of its use at these distances."

"Possibly not, but it's the best tool we have under the circumstances," Magnus pointed out. "Using ordinary radio we would sit out several lifetimes waiting for an answer."

"I think we should try again. It could be that the message was incorrectly beamed, that it hasn't got through to Earth at all."

"I hardly think that Lieutenant Maranne would be likely to make such an elementary mistake," Magnus said. "She strikes me as being a very efficient young woman. However, if there is no reply of any kind within the next two hours, then perhaps it would be a good idea to send the message again."

Piet Huygens sat alone in his cabin that was now a cell, thinking of Mia who was many miles away in the small town of Nisuno . . . Mia, whom he had deserted in the hour of her greatest need.

At the time it had not seemed like desertion. When he had seen the monstrous creature to which she had given birth, he had acted reflexively, knowing that it was his duty to take this thing back to *Venturer Twelve*. Now . . . he was beginning to have doubts.

The door of the cabin opened, breaking in abruptly on his train of self-recrimination. The visitor was Leela De Witt. Closing the door behind her, she stood, looking down at him, a half-smile on her thin-featured face.

"Hallo, Piet," she said quietly. "How goes it?"

"I left her," he said. "After all she'd gone through, I just up and left her."

"You did what you had to do," said Leela De Witt. "Thanks to you, we at least know what's going on on this planet at last."

"Like I did my duty, as a Corps officer?"

"Well, didn't you?"

He shrugged hopelessly. "That's only one way of looking at it, isn't it?"

"There's another?"

"Of course there is, you know damned well there is," he said, bitterly. "Faced with a situation I couldn't handle, I came running back to *Vee Twelve* and the Corps—like a kid howling *Mamma!*"

"That happens to us all at some time or another," De Witt said calmly.

"To you?"

"Maybe not today, or tomorrow, but sometime it could."

He looked at her steadily. He had always liked De Witt, respected her. She at least appeared more human than the average run of Corps officer, more understanding . . . or maybe that was just her stock in trade as a psyche specialist. Or maybe it was that she was married to Han De Witt, astrogation officer.

"It was a dream," he said. "We were going to escape

from the Corps, live a new, fulfilled life, just one man and one woman who loved each other. But the dream went sour. Maybe if I'd been able to work, to contribute something. . . . But even then, I'd never have fitted in. They're Mia's people on Kepler III, but they could never have been mine. And now, because of what I did, I don't fit in here, either, do I?"

"Nonsense!" she said, with a touch of sharpness. "You know what 'fitting in' means? It means being needed, having some useful function, doing the job you've been trained to do."

"And you seriously believe that Bruce will ever give me that opportunity?"

"He'll *have* to," she said. "If Maseba's program is to go through—and there is no reasonable alternative—then we shall need every ounce of medical skill we can lay our hands on. A million people to be subjected to complete genetic analysis, a million people to be given immunization shots of an attenuated virus that hasn't even been developed yet. And we've got to do it alone, with the resources at our disposal now, because it will take at least four months for a ship to get here from Earth, and by then it may be too late."

He looked at her, his spirits lightening slightly at the thought of immersing himself in useful activity, then his face clouded again. "And Mia . . .?"

"Tell us where she is, and we'll have her back here within a couple of hours," said Leela De Witt. "I'll personally guarantee that you'll be given an opportunity to talk to her alone, to explain why you did what you did."

"Do you honestly think she'd listen—even if I were capable of explaining?"

"If she loves you—yes, I think she would."

"Love . . . I wonder if there really is such a thing? Maybe it's just an itch in the crotch after all, just the idea of having something different, with a different woman . . ."

"You know that's not true," she said.

"Do I?" He stared at her with eyes dulled by the anguish inside him.

"Tell me where she is, and you'll have the opportunity of finding out."

He shook his head. "No. If she wants to come back here—to me—then that has to be her decision. I've betrayed her sufficiently already."

Lieutenant Yvonne Maranne was twenty-three years old, dark-haired and coffee-skinned, with bedroom eyes and a curvy-curvy body that set crewmen dreaming unattainable dreams. She also had sufficient intelligence to know when to use these assets; and this was not one of those times. Facing Commander Tom Bruce, across his desk, her hair drawn back severely and her face completely innocent of cosmetic aids, she looked almost plain. Almost . . . reflected Charles Magnus, reminiscently; because for him, at least, it had been proved that there was a great deal more to Yvonne Maranne than met the eye on official occasions such as this.

"Well, lieutenant?" demanded Bruce, his lean face stony.

"We've done a complete checkover of the sub-etheric installation, and as far as we can ascertain both transmission and reception facilities are in perfect order," said Maranne.

"Then why haven't we had any reply from Earth?"

"It is possible that our transmissions are being deliberately jammed, by some kind of force-barrier through which such sub-etheric waves are incapable of passing."

"Is there any way of verifying this?" Bruce said, his face darkening.

"There would be if we were in space," Maranne said.

"We could send out a Centaur Fifteen equipped with a small sub-etheric transmitter and trace it by radar. That would at least tell us if and where such a barrier exists."

"How long would it take you to prepare such a rig?"

"Twenty-four hours, maybe."

"Right, lieutenant—I want it ready in fifteen," snapped Bruce. "Now—move!"

When Maranne was gone, he turned to look at Magnus. "You realize what this means? They're out there, beyond the range of our radar, waiting and watching. And we are effectively isolated, cut off from Earth and any hope of assistance. Why haven't they attacked?"

"I think Ichiwara would answer that question by saying something like: 'When a farmer finds a fox in his chickens, he does not retaliate by burning down the henhouse,'" said Magnus. "After all, as far as the Kilroys are aware, Kepler III holds some valuable experimental breeding stock."

"You're suggesting that as long as we stay planet-bound they won't attack?"

"That seems to be a possibility," Magnus said. "On the other hand, once *Venturer Twelve* takes to space, they may very well close in."

"In that case, the sooner we get off this planet the better," Bruce said.

"To face an unknown enemy—with God knows what weapons at his disposal?" Magnus said. "You're very eager for this confrontation, Commander."

"You've only seen the pictures," Bruce said, his voice trembling with a barely controlled rage. "I was there on Minos IV. Sometimes I wake up at nights even now, seeing them, smelling the stench of them and hearing the sound of their cries. I destroyed them, out of mercy, every last one of them, but when I did, I vowed to myself that if ever the chance came, I'd exact revenge on the race that created them."

Magnus sighed. "Very well, Commander. You may prepare for liftoff at sixteen hundred hours tomorrow evening. That will give me time to make the necessary preparations."

Bruce frowned. "Preparations?"

"The Keplerian people will have to be given some plausible reason for the ship's leaving at this stage. I shall tell President Kido that you are taking her out into space in order to carry out routine repairs and tests on the main drive units. That and the presence of myself should convince him that at least he and his people are not being deserted."

"You're going to stay here, on Kepler?"

"But of course—my place is here, until the conclusion of the independence investigation, at any rate," Magnus said calmly. "In any case, I'm afraid that my presence aboard *Venturer* in the event of a confrontation with the Kilroys would be highly undesirable, and a distraction to you in the efficient performance of your duty. As the senior Corps officer in the area, any such matter of alien contact is your responsibility according to protocol."

Bruce stared at the Explorations Divison officer. "Don't you even want to know my intended plans, in the event of contact?"

"No, Commander. You are, in your own words, 'the man on the spot,' and you must have a completely free hand."

Bruce found himself looking on Magnus with a new respect. There had been times in the past when he had found what he took to be the man's arrogant assumption of his own powers a considerable irritant. Now he was able to see that behavior from a different angle, to understand that a great deal of what he had mistaken for arrogance was in fact calm conviction, and rigid adherence to principles understood and respected.

"And the Keplerians are to be told nothing?" he said.

"There would be no useful purpose in alarming them at this stage," Magnus said. "As far as they are concerned, the independence investigation must appear to be going ahead as planned. And, of course, the work on the elimination of Johannsen's disease. Surgeon Lieutenant Maseba must continue with his research program, and be seen to do so. Such activity will maintain the confidence of the Keplerians in our intentions."

"Maseba!" Bruce stiffened. "You mean you expect me to leave my chief medical officer here on Kepler, while I take this ship into action against an unknown enemy?"

"It is essential that Maseba should remain," Magnus said. "He is already well-known to the Keplerians. As for the running of the medical section aboard ship, you have his deputy, De Witt, a very efficient young woman—and there is, of course, our young friend Huygens."

"Huygens!" grunted Bruce. "A blasted disgrace to the Corps."

"An unwise young man, no doubt, in many ways," Magnus said. "But a competent medic, I understand, who could prove useful in an emergency."

"Huygens stays in close arrest," snapped Bruce. "As far as I'm concerned, he is no longer capable of being entrusted with the duties of a medical officer."

Tom Bruce's green eyes narrowed as he looked into the ebony features of Surgeon Lietutenant George Maseba. "What the hell is this—some kind of conspiracy? When did you join the Let's-be-kind-to-Piet-Huygens Society?"

"Nobody's being kind—this is just common sense," said Maseba.

Bruce rose jerkily from behind the desk and strode about the office as he talked. "Common sense, is it? A deserter, in close arrest, awaiting court martial, we let him out of his cell with a gentle slap on the wrist, and put him back down on the very planet where he deserted in the first place—where, I might add, his partner-in-crime is still at large. Jesus H. Christ, George! What kind of stupid move is that? He'll be off like a bloody rabbit as soon as he sets foot on the ground. Apart from that—look at the disciplinary aspect. What will the rest of the crew think?"

"They'll think what you tell them to," Maseba said, doggedly. "Huygens will be released into my custody, as senior medical officer. I'll accept full responsibility for him."

"Well that's just dandy!" snapped Bruce. "So what do I do when he decides to go over the wall again— put you on a charge, too?"

"He's not going any place, but into a laboratory, where he'll be working harder than he ever has in his life," said Maseba. "We're both agreed that Leela De Witt must stay aboard *Vee Twelve* when you lift off. It would be suicidal to take the ship into action without at least one competent medical officer aboard. That means that I shall be left here on Kepler with half a dozen orderlies and a handful of colonial-trained hick doctors to tackle a medical emergency situation involving a population of a million people. Whatever you may think of him personally and as a Corps officer, I need Huygens. After passing his finals he worked for two whole years in virology research back in Lake Cities, before joining the Corps. In my present situation, his knowledge could be invaluable."

"How do you know he would be prepared to cooperate?"

"De Witt has talked to him several times since his return. She's of the opinion that immersion in such work would have considerable therapeutic value for him, from the psyche point of view."

Bruce looked at his chief medical officer long and

hard. "All right, George. We'll do it your way. Just keep the bastard out of my sight, that's all."

"Will do, Commander," Maseba said, with a grin. He turned to leave.

"Oh, and George . . ." Bruce said.

"Commander?"

"Tell De Witt to let me have that psyche recommendation of hers in writing, will you? Just for the record."

If there was ever a color for sorrow, it was not blue, as the African peoples claimed; it was gray. Mia Mizuno knew it, felt it throughout her whole being. Physically, she was an attractive and healthy young woman who had accomplished the task of giving birth with complete satisfaction. Spiritually, she was in a condition not far removed from death. Not an hour passed but she reviewed with non-understanding sadness this incredible thing which had happened to her. For a fortnight she had been in a trancelike state from which, even now, she was only emerging with reluctance. That bright, gay, passionate Mia no longer existed, and to Jiro Osuragi it seemed possible that never again would her mind be unclouded.

Doctor Osuragi and his sister, who was matron of the little clinic, had been kindness personified. They made her a guest in their apartment, spoke gently to her, looked after her in every possible way. When, momentarily, she had come out of her sorrow to express the wish that she should get some work, Osuragi had got on at once to a friend who was personnel manager of the local Akai electronics factory, to see what might be done for her; but almost directly after, he had to cancel a provisional appointment, because

Mia was not fit to take up the threads of a life which was without Piet Huygens.

Without Piet . . . without Piet . . . that was the problem.

Osuragi and his sister could help little in giving reasons for Piet's departure.

Now she sat in her plain but dainty little room, with folded hands and aching mind, and wondered. Piet had left her; he had meant nothing when he said he loved her; at most, he was trying to reshape his past into a shape which was less haunting to his constricted inner self.

Her eye caught a newspaper . . . "The Magnificent Work of the Medical Staff of *Venturer Twelve.* . . ." Oh, yes. *Venturer Twelve.* Crewwoman—no, Leading Crewwoman Mizuno. The girl they would leave behind them. She looked at the television set, then back at the paper. Channel eight, formerly reserved for ancient ritual and culture programs, reports three times a day on the work of the medical unit whose efforts mean life and death for us all. . . .

She switched on the set, and pressed a button for channel eight. A serious-faced commentator filled the screen. "Using special drugs, the key men of this important enterprise are able to cut down their sleep to six hours per day out of the twenty-eight; for the rest of the time, except for short meal breaks, they work as the spearhead of our own doctors. Now, we bring you a very short interview with one of these selfless scientists. Be proud to meet Lieutenant Piet Huygens."

Then she saw him; his face was thinner, he looked tired out, but he was her Piet—and he had gone back to fight this . . . what was it? A disease which threatened Kepler III. . . . It didn't matter. There was her Piet. She knew where he was. She must go to him. She must go to him. There would be reasons why he had left her. Piet still loved her, she knew, she *knew!*

He was her man. She would find him, come what may.

Lieutenant Wiltrud Anna Hoffman, the sleek lines of the scout ship looming behind her, stood on Rokoa field and looked up into the night sky of Kepler III. Out there, somewhere, *Venturer Twelve* was hunting for the unseen enemy; out there, history was being made, the first face-to-face encounter of mankind and alien . . . an encounter feared and yet in some curious way looked forward to . . . one which would give meaning to all the training, the armament of such ships as *Vee Twelve*. And she . . . ? Her training, her life . . . devoted to the Corps and its aims . . . a good officer, with ability and determination . . . she was not even to be a spectator to this confrontation. . . . Her job was to wait here, on Rokoa field, to wait for an indefinite period, and eventually to provide transport for Maseba and Magnus back to *Vee Twelve*.

A warm breeze blowing across the field tangled her short-cut blonde hair, and she moved her hand up irritably to brush it back from her forehead. Behind her, through the open airlock, she could hear the subdued murmur of a radio in the crew quarters. Tuned to a local Kepler station, it was playing the kind of weird, archaic chamber-jazz favored by the Keplerians. There were two crewmen, besides herself and P.O. Patel, with the scout ship—and so she, as an officer, was to all intents, alone. Alone and bored. Her eyes moved restlessly, looking beyond the perimeter of the field, towards the lights of the suburb of Shamari. There at least, people were living, there was excitement, human contact of some kind. . . . A Corps officer might find interesting ways of diverting herself, of relieving a boredom that threatened to. . . . But then, there were other aspects to be considered—the appearance of a Corps officer in Shamari at this time would certainly be remarked upon; on the other hand . . .

The idea that struck her contained all the elements necessary to combat her ennui, carrying as it did, simultaneously, the appeal of both the known and the unknown—and at the same time an element of safety from the Corps disciplinary point of view. Moving with new determination, she walked back up the ramp to the control cabin of the ship. P.O. Patel, brown and stockily built, was seated by the sub-etheric. He moved to his feet as she entered.

"I'm taking one of the ground cars over to the Medical Inspection Center," she said.

Patel's Eastern bumpkin face showed no change of expression. "Yes, ma'am. If anything comes through from *Vee Twelve?*"

She patted the side pocket of her tunic. "You can get me anytime you like—I have my personal communicator.

"Ma'am." Patel nodded. "When will you be back?"

"I'm not sure. It may be morning," she said. "Carry on, P.O." Without waiting for his answer, she turned and headed back down the ramp towards the ground car park.

The Combat Information Display of *Venturer Twelve* gave a God's-eye view, and Tom Bruce, seated in his command position at the console of the Combat Control Computer, was God, looking down on the enormous tank-screen which presented a three-dimensional picture of space up to a range of half a light year. Translating the information from the ship's myriad exterior sensors, radar, video camera, gravity and radiation field detectors, CID showed *Venturer Twelve* at the center of a display which took in the entirety of the Kepler sun system, with Kepler III a blue-green ball flanked by its satellites just off to the left. Beyond that lay the two barren rocky spheres of the inner planets; and farther away still, the Kepler sun itself, its blue-white brilliance damped down by the display to a more tolerable intensity.

Godlike too, was the tremendous destructive power represented by the controls beneath Bruce's fingertips, which were capable of releasing the massive armament of this, United Earth's largest and most advanced ship, armament capable of reducing a medium-size planet to a boiling mass of radioactive matter within a few minutes. Mankind had been preparing for this moment for over a century, and now, at last, here in this remote corner of the universe, fifteen parsecs from Earth, possibility was becoming reality. And Bruce was the man on the spot—Bruce, with his extension the Combat Control Computer, which could think faster, calculate with greater accuracy than any living creature, and was thus capable of making the necessary decisions in the four-dimensional chess game that was war in space.

Maranne's voice: "Missile proceeding, on course. Transmission normal . . . Approaching speed .25 light and holding. . . ."

The Centaur Fifteen missile was shown on CID as a small dot, creeping along the green dotted line that was its predicted trajectory. A loudspeaker over Bruce's head relayed the continuous beep-beep transmitted by the small sub-etheric transmitter installed by Maranne's section in the heart of the missile.

Bruce, conscious of the smell of his own sweat, shifted slightly in his well-padded seat, and wondered, how long? How long before the missile made contact with the invisible barrier of radiation that had prevented *Venturer*'s sub-etheric message from getting through to Earth? How long, and how far behind the barrier was the ship or ships, which had erected that barrier—the ships controlled by the unseen, long-awaited enemy, the creatures whose tracks had bred the Kilroy legend, whose handiwork he had seen there on the raped planet of Minos IV, and here on Kepler where they had altered the very seed of man? Wherever they were, those ships were still too far away to show up on any of *Venturer*'s detectors. Waiting there . . . for what?

"Fifteen million kilometers out, still on course." Maranne's voice again.

Beside him he could sense, at the periphery of his vision, the presence of Helen Lindstrom. She too would be watching the display, knowing what this moment meant to him, to all of mankind.

Beep-beep-beep-beep . . . regular, metronomic, the measured pulse of the Centaur missile's transmitter.

All over *Venturer Twelve* men stood at battle stations, watching screens, armament prepared, awaiting orders . . .

Beep-beep-bee . . .

Bruce sat, straining his ears for the next in the sequence, and there was a deadly quiet throughout the ship's tactical nerve center as everyone else did the same.

Transmission from the missile had ceased.

And yet, looking down into the CID tank-screen, the red dot of the Centaurus Fifteen still showed, climbing steadily up the ladder of green dots. It remained for almost a full minute, then flared briefly into incandescence and was gone.

Bruce knew that in reality the missile had died at the moment its transmission had ceased, and that the red dot in the CID had been a ghost, caused by the lagging snail-pace of radar and light waves as compared with sub-etheric. Galvanizing into action, he began to feed instructions into the battle computer. Instantaneously, under the direct control of the computer, the intensity of the ship's huge Grenbach drives began to increase, thrusting her forward with mounting acceleration, following the trajectory of the missile, plunging towards the unknown. . . .

Piet Huygens lay naked on his bed in the Medical Inspection Center, waiting for a sleep that refused to come. Despite air-conditioning, the air of the small room was hot and thick. Throughout the day there had been no time for external thought—he had been immersed in work, work of the kind he understood, for which he had been trained; cultures, tissue samples, the moving, tiny worlds of virus and bacteria viewed through a microscope. But now, once again, there was time to think, and he was haunted by the shadows of his guilt, and thoughts of Mia, so many miles away.

Perhaps it would have been best to have told them where she was, so that she could be brought back, but to do that would have been somehow compounding his first betrayal of her. He wanted Mia—but not as a prisoner. He wondered what she had been doing since his flight from Nisuno. Was she still there in Osuragi's small clinic? Had she decided to try to make some kind of life for herself among those people? Perhaps hoping vainly that he would one day return to her? Or had she cut herself off from him with a barrier of hate and resentment for his desertion of her? Was it possible that her love could have turned to hate?

Outside the building he heard the purring of a ground car engine approaching, then stopping. Someone else, who like himself was unable to sleep? No, no one else could carry such a burden of guilt.

He wondered briefly if he should go back to the laboratory and continue his work—there at least there would be something to occupy his mind, to banish the shadows. He dismissed the idea almost as soon as it was formed. He was tired, beyond that point where he could work efficiently, and tomorrow there would be more and more for him to do. Tomorrow Doctor Osawa, Sato's assistant, would be joining him, and they would begin the task of correlating their results. Osawa had been working on the problem for some time, and there was just a chance that her information might be valuable. If he was to be fresh and alert for that meeting, he must have sleep, now. . . .

Swinging his legs over the edge of the bed, he rose to his feet and walked over to the wash basin. He drew off a glass of water, and was standing with the two yellow sleeping pills in his left hand, when there was a light tap on the door.

"Come in," he spoke reflexively, without thinking.

She entered the room quietly, closing the door behind her and leaning against it as she stood looking at him. "Hallo, Piet," she said, her ice-blue eyes glinting. "Sleeping pills? You won't be needing them, now."

"Trudi! What the hell do you want?" He put the pills and glass down on the washbasin, conscious of the curious prudery of the action as his hands moved awkwardly to cover his nakedness.

She moved towards him, her moist lips smiling. "What did I ever want?"

"With me? After what's happened?"

"Of course, with you—we suit each other, remember?" she said, tense, a tigress in heat. Her hand trembled as she unzipped her tunic.

"But me . . . my seed . . . the Johannsen's. . . ." He could feel the coolness of the washbasin against his bare buttocks.

"Christ! What's the matter with you? You used to like it as much and as often as me. I don't want to breed with you, for God's sake!"

"No Trudi—Leave me alone!"

"Leave me alone!" she mimicked him, contemptuously. "You're not still thinking about that little monkey woman, are you? You'll never see her again. Come

to think of it, you won't get a lot of opportunities where you're going, will you? They don't cater much for sexual athletes in Earthside jails, as far as I hear . . . better make the most of what you can get now, eh?"

"No—I don't want you—how many times?" He grabbed a towel from the rail by the basin, and draped it about his waist.

She stood, one hand paused on the zip of her trousers, and laughed with a sudden harshness. "Oh, no! It's just occurred to me. Maybe you're not still pining for your little yellow whore at all—maybe you just can't do it any more—is that it?"

"What are you talking about?"

"You mean you don't know? You're so mixed up with your bloody microscopes and cultures you haven't heard? No, perhaps he didn't think it would be a good idea to tell you. . . ."

He moved forward, propelled by his anger, his hands grasping at the firm flesh of her shoulders. "What the hell are you talking about?" he demanded, shaking her.

"Well, it's obvious, isn't it? People like you—and all the rest of those with this thing in their genetic structure. They can't be allowed to breed. . . . ever, can they? What do you think this examination program of Maseba's is for, anyway? Those—the ones who are found defective genetically, they aren't just going to get a shot of anti-Johannsen's serum; they'll have to be permanently sterilized, because there's no way of changing them back."

It made sense . . . of course, it was the only way Maseba could tackle the problem. There could be no more monster births . . . that much was obvious. Memory flooded back into his mind, combining with his tiredness, and her hate-filled contemptuous voice . . .

"Maseba's been there already with his scalpel, hasn't he?" she said, spitting the words in his face, her blue eyes flaring with contempt. "Is that it? Did I come too late for the party? *You bloody eunuch!*"

The word pierced through the confusion of his mind, a burning torch thrust into the straw of his frustration, and erupted into a flaming rage that demanded physical release. She was a strong, fit woman, with a big, athletic body, but before such fury she was helpless.

When at last he was able to think clearly again, his rage burned out, she was lying, her body crumpled in an awkward, doll-like position, beneath the washbasin, the ice-blue eyes still open, staring up at him.

Bending down beside her, he begged her forgiveness. "Trudi, I don't know. . . ." His hand behind her head . . . felt the pulpy softness of a smashed skull, and he stopped, knowing beyond doubt that she was dead, the raging ache of her loins ceased forever.

Rinsing the blood from his hands, he began to dress quickly. His doubts, his uncertainties were gone now. Her death had resolved the situation—pointed at him the only possible way in which he could go. Certainly, whatever happened now he could never return to *Vee Twelve*. As a murderer, he was a certain candidate for complete psyche erasure and reconditioning. There was no appeal. And even though the fact of being Piet Huygens was, had been, agony, anything was preferable to the idea that Piet Huygens, as Piet Huygens, should cease to exist.

Pausing only to take the keys of Trudi's ground car from the pocket of her tunic, he hurried out of the building. He knew where he was going, and there was no alternative. The ground car purred into life, and he steered it out onto the highway.

"Mia, love, I'm coming back, Mia . . ." he murmured as the car gathered speed.

"Point four-five light," said Lindstrom's voice at his elbow. "In ten seconds we shall be at the point where the Centaurus missile was destroyed."

Ten seconds, nine, five . . . Bruce felt them slip away from him, draining away like drops of his life-blood. His hands moving over the console keys, he demanded information, but on the screens above the CID nothing showed. Tuned to their farthest limits the ship sensors could still not detect the presence of the aliens. And yet they must be there, somewhere . . .

The words of Kavanin's poem rattled crazily in his head: *But they are there somewhere. . . . They have to be. By all the laws of probability* . . .

Soon they must be within effective range—the destruction of the missile demanded that it should be so. But that effective range—was Kilroy effective range so much farther than that of *Venturer?* Could they remain out there, beyond reach of the Earth ship's sensors, and still destroy her?

Three seconds . . . two . . . one . . .

"My God! Look at that!" Lindstrom's voice was a strangled gasp, her arm pointed to the heart of the CID display.

There, way over to the left-hand side of the tank, close by the blue-green ball of Kepler III, was something like a great, luminous jellyfish. It hung there, its brilliance pulsing up and down the spectrum, its size indeterminate.

Bruce fingered the keys swiftly, punching his instructions into the computer, and a moment later an enlarged view of the thing appeared in an auxiliary screen above the CID. It appeared to be an amorphous mass, brilliant in its luminosity, a flickering mirage that strained the capacity of the human optical faculties.

"Phasing in," Lindstrom said. "They must be using some kind of warp drive. Probably takes them some time to stabilize when they surface into 'true' space."

Cool, efficient, for all her woman's weaknesses, thought Bruce. Faced by the situation every Corpsman had dreaded since the beginning, she could still remain analytical. Warp drive—talked of in theory, but never yet realized; based on the idea that in another, subspatial dimension, some kind of Möbius principle might exist, under which the shortest distance between two points was no longer a straight line, but a mere step in a new, as yet inconceivable 'direction.' A now-you-see-it-now-you-don't kind of conjuring trick, it was the only explanation that could account for the fact of the Kilroy ship being at one moment twenty million kilometers from Kepler III, and at the next, hovering in orbit a mere thousand kilometers above the planet.

And twenty million kilometers away from *Venturer Twelve,* in the opposite direction—with the distance increasing at a speed of point four-seven light.

"Grav field detectors indicate a mass in excess of two million tons," said Lindstrom.

Bruce made no reply. He was fully occupied feeding his instructions into the battle computer. Even as the ship went into the screaming arc of a turn, overloading the compensating grav circuits to maximum, he experienced a feeling of impotence in the knowledge that coming to grips with such an enemy might well be an impossibility. With such a drive, long before *Venturer,* moving at her maximum speed, could come within range, the alien could once again "submerge" into subspace and be several million miles away.

In the auxiliary screen the image of the Kilroy ship was stabilized now, a vast, black elliptical shape, ringed by a corona of purple, close in on the night side of Kepler III.

And on the planet itself, rapidly growing, like the replication of some monstrous disease, spots of incandescence.

"They're attacking Kepler III!" Lindstrom said, superfluously.

Bruce had already seen, and understood what was happening. He had been decoyed out into deep space, and now the very planet he was supposed to be protecting was at the mercy of the enemy.

"Contact Hoffman," he shouted to Maranne. "Tell her to get all personnel aboard the scout ship immediately, and get to hell out of there!" *If it isn't already too late,* his mind added, as the moving sores of incandescence spread over the surface of the planet.

George Maseba was at the wheel of the leading ground car, with Caiola in the seat beside him. Behind, in convoy, was the rest of the medic team—except for Piet Huygens. Bruce would gripe about that, especially when he heard that he had lost Hoffman as well. Poor, over-sexed bitch! Maseba blamed himself partly, for not having insisted on giving her compulsory hormone-balancing therapy. The idea had occurred to him in the past, but there had always been something more important to demand his attention, and now . . . now it was too late.

"God! Look at that!" exclaimed Caiola, pointing over to the east, where a false, leprous dawn was breaking as columns of roiling fire leaped upwards.

"Emergency Sky Bolt! Emergency Sky Bolt! All Corps personnel report to Rokoa field immediately for scramble liftoff! Emergency Sky Bolt! Emergency Sky Bolt! All . . ." P.O. Patel's voice still rattled small in the communicator propped above the dashboard of the car, awaiting no reply, just going on and on repeating the message, because to such a message there was no reply in words; it demanded nothing less than physical presence, in the shortest possible time.

The code words "Sky Bolt" meant only one thing in Corps language. Kepler III was under attack from space. And if that was the case, then the only means of escape was the one tiny scout ship, commanded now by P.O. Patel—a cockleshell, capable of holding a mere thirty people. And the other million? Maseba glanced away at the hellish, climbing fires, and tried not to think of them.

Charles Magnus stood by the doorway of the helibus, clipboard in his hand, checking as the members of his staff filed aboard, glancing occasionally across the roofs of Central City towards the east. His first reaction on being awakened by the insistent yammering of the personal communicator had been that this was yet another piece of absurd Corps melodrama, but sight of the flaming destruction which was advancing slowly on the city had quickly dissipated any doubts.

The elevator arrived at the rooftop, and discharged its cargo. Two flustered female clerks, dabbing ineffectually at their makeup, loaded down with bags and souvenirs, stumbled aboard the helibus.

"Farquhar . . . Morales . . ." Magnus ticked off the two names. "Has anyone seen Mr. Ichiwara?"

"He went to his office, sir. Something about essential files," supplied one of the men.

Ichiwara. A planet was being destroyed, and Ichiwara could only think of his precious files. Where would Earth, and Explorations Division in particular, be without such men? thought Magnus, a smile tugging at the corners of his thin lips.

He glanced at his watch. Twenty minutes since the

first alarm. Not bad timing. But how long would P.O. Patel delay his liftoff? Patel—why *Patel?* Surely that man-eating dragon Hoffman was in command of the scout ship?

An elderly secretary, hair still in rollers, looking like a disgruntled, stout porcupine, hurried aboard.

"Browning . . ." Magnus made another tick. Now only Ichiwara remained.

From the north, a sound like thunder rumbled; instantaneously, the burgeoning glow of a new fire. The city was now hemmed in on two sides.

Bruce, what the devil was the man doing? United Earth's finest ship at his command, the ship he had talked about with such pride, and yet Kepler III appeared to be totally at the mercy of the aliens. Was he perhaps outnumbered? It seemed hardly likely that he was outclassed. Although he regarded Bruce as an eminently stupid man in some ways, Magnus had the greatest respect for his ability as a commander.

The elevator doors opened again, disgorging Joseph Ichiwara, hung like a Christmas tree with briefcases and files. Smiling apologetically, he scurried with his curious pigeon-toed walk across to the helibus.

As soon as he was aboard, Magnus turned to the Kepler pilot. "All right. You can take off now."

The idling engines burst into urgent life and the helibus lifted from the roof, swinging out over the streets of the city. Although it still wanted an hour to dawn, those streets were thronged with curious, frightened people, wakened by the "thunderstorm" and mercifully still unaware of the true nature of their peril.

"I'm afraid I wasn't able to bring the Agricultural and Fisheries Reports," said Ichiwara, at his elbow. "The head of the department must have taken the key away last night."

"For this one omission you shall be duly forgiven, my dear Joseph," said Magnus, consolingly. "I somehow doubt that any of our statistics will have a great deal of validity for much longer."

The helibus sped over the threatened city towards Rokoa Field.

Maseba's convoy entered the suburb of Shimara. Lights were on in the houses, bewildered people standing in the streets, looking towards the glow in the eastern sky. Near the town square, a man threw himself towards Maseba's car, hands outstretched in vain supplication. Maseba drove doggedly on, aware of the thud of the body against the coachwork. This was no time to hesitate.

They were on the straight tarmacadam road now, leading to Rokoa Field.

"Have your needler ready, just in case," he said to Caiola.

"Ready, sir," said the orderly, as they approached the white-painted metal gates of the field.

Two guards, their weapons at the trail, stood looking towards the east, and with them, a small knot of civilians. Maseba sounded his horn, as he rolled to a stop.

He leaned out of the car window. "Surgeon Lieutenant Maseba—on official business. Open up!" he shouted.

The guards turned and hurried across at the double. One of them, little more than a boy, looked in at Maseba. "What's happening, sir?"

"Electrical storm—nothing to worry about," Maseba said curtly. "Open up those gates!"

The guard hesitated.

"Move, man! Move!" shouted Maseba, in creditable imitation of Bruce.

The guards ran towards the gate.

"Sir—that woman!" said Caiola, one hand on Maseba's arm, the other pointing towards the knot of bewildered civilians.

Maseba looked, and saw a small woman, in shapeless Keplerian coveralls, walking uncertainly towards the convoy.

"Crewwoman Mizuno!" he snapped instantly. "Get her, Caiola!"

A moment later, the gate opened, and the convoy began to roll across the field towards the waiting scout ship, with Mia Mizuno bundled in the front seat of the leading car, between Maseba and Caiola.

"Piet . . . Where is Piet?" she asked.

Over to the left of the field, Maseba saw a long, gray helibus descending.

Venturer Twelve had completed her arc now, and was heading in towards Kepler III. But the turn had taken too long. What had been a blue-green, fertile planet was now a bright new sun, burning with fearful intensity.

"My God!" whispered Lindstrom at his elbow.

"Your God doesn't live around this part of the galaxy," Bruce said, his eyes on the CID, where the Kilroy ship still showed, hovering over the stricken planet like some great black vampire bat. But he was praying himself, just the same, that the alien would remain where it was for just a few seconds more; so that it would be within range of *Vee Twelve*'s weapons as she swung past Kepler III in a space-eating parabola at point six five light.

Up on one of the auxiliary screens, white figures a foot high ticked off the seconds to contact time.

Fifteen . . . fourteen. . . . The vampire bat remained steady, gloating on its handiwork.

Bruce sat back in his command chair. There was

nothing he could do now. The outcome was in the hands of the battle computer; no human being was capable of the millisecond calculations needed to conduct such an attack.

He called to Maranne. "Anything from the scout ship?"

"No, sir. But they may be in the planet's shadow."

Nine . . . eight . . . seven. . . . The alien was still there, hovering above the ravening fires.

"If they managed to get away . . ." said Bruce, grimly; George Maseba, Magnus, their staffs. . . .

Five . . . four . . . three. . . .

The image of the alien ship began to flicker, pulsing in and out at rapidly increasing speed. It was no longer black, but acquiring luminosity as its color gradually climbed up the spectrum towards flaring white. At the same time, it appeared to increase in size.

And then, abruptly, it was gone

For the space of two heartbeats there was a great silence aboard *Venturer Twelve,* then Bruce spoke: "We call them Kilroys. It's like a joke—the worst bloody joke I ever heard." The crew of *Venturer Twelve* had never heard before such emotion in their chief's voice.

On the auxiliary screen the words NO CONTACT appeared, mocking, derisive.

The enemy had gone, carrying his secrets with him . . . once again. Bruce rose from the command chair, stretching cramped limbs.

"Scout ship calling in now," shouted Maranne.

Bruce turned to Lindstrom. "Handle it, will you?" He walked out of Battle Control, tasting the bitter ashes of defeat.

Venturer Twelve was on her way back home, but there was little joy in that thought for Tom Bruce, because the enemy had gone, and he had been cheated of the long-awaited confrontation yet again. There was no way of probing the unhuman motivation of such an opponent; no way of telling whether he had been afraid to join battle with the might of *Venturer Twelve,* or whether, his task of destroying Kepler III completed, he had decided contemptuously that the Earth ship was not worthy of his attention.

Kilroy was here and gone, back into the sanctuary of the subspatial dimension, where *Venturer* could not follow. Perhaps even now the alien ship was homing in on its parent solar system, wherever that might be. With the going of the alien ship, the sub-etheric barrier between *Venturer Twelve* and Earth no longer existed, and the report of the abortive encounter could be transmitted, along with a message urging the interception of the ore ship *Wangituru* before she could land on Earth, and her crew could spread the genetic poison of the Kilroy-mutated Johannsen's virus. At the price of a million lives, and the loss of an entire planet, that danger, at least, had been averted.

Ridden by the bitter inconclusiveness of the situation, Bruce was an angry, intolerant man as he faced Surgeon Lieutenant George Maseba.

"I don't believe you!" he snapped. "Flatly and finally, I don't believe you! And when it comes to the point I can categorically refuse your request."

Maseba faced him stolidly. "Very well, sir, I shall have to enter it in my records that you have refused a priority recommendation for medical treatment—treatment that I consider to be necessary."

Bruce put his hands flat on his desk, his mouth a

tight line. "In my book, what you're suggesting doesn't constitute any normal type of medical treatment."

"Neither is this a normal situation," Maseba pointed out.

"You're splitting hairs, Lieutenant! Can't you see that you're asking me to compound a major disciplinary crime?"

"De Witt and I will both sign the recommendation, sir."

"I don't care if Hippocrates himself signs the damned thing—I'll countersign it—PERMISSION REFUSED."

"In that case, I would like permission to talk direct with the surgeon general of the Corps on sub-etheric. Do you refuse that, sir?"

"No."

"Thank you, sir."

Bruce compressed his exasperation into a manageable size. "You really are serious, aren't you?"

Maseba stared hard, and showed the brown-flecked whites of his eyes. "I thought you'd gathered that." He added, with an almost pleading note. "For God's sake, sir, let's come out of this thing with at least one tiny piece of credit balance on the human side. At least, see her."

Bruce seemed about to speak, and then didn't.

"Please."

Bruce sighed. "All right. I'll see her."

"And be kind to her."

"Is that an order, Surgeon Lieutenant?"

Maseba shook his head slowly. "No—just a recommendation." He moved towards the door. "Shall I bring her in?"

"Send her in," Bruce growled. "I'll handle this my way. Your part comes afterwards."

Mia Mizuno forced herself to be calm as she stood in her number twos in front of the steel desk in the drab gray room and faced the man who had spoken to her only once during all the time she had been a member of *Venturer Twelve*'s crew. Tell the truth, Leela De Witt had said, and answer every question he asks loud and clear.

She had never really looked at Bruce before; he had been someone far away and above her, and all he had ever required of Leading Crewwoman Mizuno in the past was that she did her duty quietly and efficiently. Now it was all different, and she did look at him. She saw a lean, hard man, one meter eighty, with graying reddish hair, flinty green eyes, and a sharp nose. A man with just a touch of sad weariness about him, despite the punctilious manner in which he returned her salute.

"At ease, Mizuno."

She obeyed, and he sat looking at her. But she did not feel uncomfortable, because she knew somehow that this man, too, had his problems, that he also was flesh and blood.

"I can't say I've ever noticed you before."

"No, sir."

"It comes of expecting everyone to do their duty, Mizuno."

"Yes, sir."

"And it comes of carrying out regulations. Regulations aren't there for fun. They're a product of the accumulated experience of the entire Corps."

"Yes, sir."

"I take it that you have no misunderstanding about the seriousness of your crime? Desertion, woman, that's the name for it."

"Yes, sir." His poor face . . . . She wondered how and where he got that livid scar on his left cheek.

"I have no power to reduce the actual charge of desertion in any way. It stands on your record, and will continue to stand permanently. Is that clear?"

She heard herself say that it was clear to her—but really, she was thinking of Piet.

For half a minute he sat, looking at her, then he rose and came closer. "But you—how do you feel about what you did? How do you feel now?"

"I am sorry to have—offended, sir."

"Sorry . . ." he repeated the word, seeming to turn it over and examine it. Then he pointed to a chair. "Sit down."

She hesitated. This was not quite what she had expected. Then she obeyed.

"Now, listen to me," he said. "I keep to regulations, and only to regulations. But regulations are not without humanity, and I am advised by my medical officers that you are a case for special treatment, which they suggest, I may authorize. But first I want your frank answers to some questions."

Now that she was seated, he seemed to tower over her, and she felt the beginnings of fear. As if sensing this, he moved away, and spoke with his back towards her.

"Mizuno, could you stand never seeing Earth again, if—if the reasons—the inducement—were big enough?"

She felt her heart leap. Maseba had been close as a clam, but Leela De Witt had hinted . . . "Yes, sir— I could."

"As you know, we are on our way back to Earth, but on our way we shall be calling at Oharo IV, a planet largely populated by people of your own ethnic group. I am told that, in the interests of your health, an appropriate discharge can and should be arranged, to take effect when we arrive at Oharo IV. Also, I am informed that your psycho-physical balance could be totally restored by one other thing." He turned and came to her, and now there was an almost gentle note in his voice. "You lost a baby—but as you have now been pronounced genetically sound, it would be possible for you to have another; your husband's child, if you so wish."

The tiny singing in her heart that had been there ever since Leela De Witt had spoken to her could no longer be contained. She sprang to her feet, crying aloud with joy.

And Bruce snapped at her. "All right. All right. Lieutenant Maseba will see to it. He tells me that it will be a simple matter to inseminate you with Huygens seed from the ship's sperm bank. Now dismiss—I've more important matters to attend to."

She saluted, and left the room. And when she was gone, he stood, still staring at the blank door, and wishing to God that all the problems of the universe might have such a simple solution.

There was no one in the corridor outside. She leaned against the wall with her eyes closed, murmuring to herself.

"Hello, little gel. Are they being nice to you, then?"

She opened her eyes. It was P.O. Dockridge. She smiled at his friendly, terrier face, but she did not speak to him. What she did was to whisper, again and again: "Oh, Piet, Piet love . . . Piet, I shall have your child."

ABOUT DAN MORGAN

DAN MORGAN is the author of eight science fiction novels—five of which have been published in the United States—and a highly successful book on the guitar, which has been selling in the United States and the United Kingdom for the past six years. He has written numerous science fiction short stories, and one previous collaborative novel with John Kippax, *Thunder of Stars,* published by Ballantine Books.

Mr. Morgan divides his time between Spalding, Lincolnshire, in flat and fertile East Anglia, and Almeria in Andalucia, which he describes as the Hollywood of Spain, and a land of spectacularly rugged mountains and sunshine. "Spain," he writes, "remains one of the few places on our planet where it is possible to live the *dulce vida* on the earnings of a science fiction writer without going broke."

Dan Morgan's hobbies are skin-diving, fish-watching, and playing the guitar—jazz, classical, and flamenco—and he likes wine, good food, and good conversation.

ABOUT JOHN KIPPAX

John Kippax, ex-schoolmaster and ex-soldier, has written most forms of fiction, including works for TV and radio (the latter being still very much a popular medium in Britain). At one time, he and Dan Morgan played guitar together, and from the musical association came the writing collaboration; despite the fact that they shared the responsibility for three of the "Venturer Twelve" series, they are still good friends, "even though we often work in reciprocal acrimony," Mr. Kippax writes. His hobbies are music—a wide variety including Ives, Copland, Ellington, and Bach—beer (at 55 degrees Fahrenheit), Chinese food, and arguing. His favorite sports team is the Harlem Globetrotters. John Kippax lives in Peterborough, England, which is nearly shouting distance from Dan Morgan's home in Spalding, and, he says, they give their opinions of each other's work with appalling bluntness.

For a complete list or to order by mail, write to
Dept. CS, Ballantine Books, 36 West 20th Street,
New York, N.Y. 10003

THE TAR-AIYM KRANG

by

Alan Dean Foster

The Planet Moth . . .

so named because of its beautiful "wings"—
great golden clouds forever suspended in space.

And like its namesake, the planet attracted un-
wary travelers—a teeming, constantly shifting
horde that provided a comfortable income for
certain quick-witted fellows like Flinx, who was
experienced in extra-legal and nefarious means
of accomplishing his ends. Yet not even Flinx
held the real key to the ultimate power of the
Krang—an artifact older than time and still
functioning . . .

95¢

*The latest collection from one of the
top ten science fiction writers*

THE REALITY TRIP
AND OTHER IMPLAUSIBILITIES

by
Hugo and Nebula Award Winner

ROBERT SILVERBERG

Eight stories of remarkably high caliber, including
the short novel, *Hawksbill Station*—stories distinguished by the sardonic quality of Silverberg's
writing, an acid wit, and a generally cerebral approach to science fiction—stories which are a positive joy to read.

95¢

For a complete list or to order by mail, write to
Dept. CS, Ballantine Books, 36 West 20th Street,
New York, N.Y. 10003